RA

Stephen Gilbert was _____, __. Down in 1912. He was sent to England for boarding school from age 10 to 13 and afterwards to a Scottish public school, which he left without passing any exams or obtaining a leaving certificate. He returned to Belfast, where he worked briefly as a journalist before joining his father's tea and seed business. In 1931, just before his nineteenth birthday, Gilbert met novelist Forrest Reid, by that time in his mid-fifties. Reid's novels reflect his lifelong fascination with boys, and he was quickly drawn to Gilbert; the two commenced a sometimes turbulent friendship that lasted until Reid's death in 1947. Reid acted as mentor to Gilbert, who had literary aspirations, and ultimately depicted an idealized version of their relationship in the novel *Brian Westby* (1934).

Gilbert's first novel, *The Landslide* (1943), a fantasy involving prehistoric creatures which appear in a remote part of Ireland after being uncovered by a landslide, appeared to generally positive reviews and was dedicated to Reid. A second novel, *Bombardier* (1944), followed, based on Gilbert's experiences in the Second World War. Gilbert's third novel, *Monkeyface* (1948), concerns what seems to be an ape, called 'Bimbo', discovered in South America and brought back to Belfast, where it learns to talk. *The Burnaby Experiments* appeared in 1952, five years after Reid's death, and is a thinly disguised portrayal of their relationship from Gilbert's point of view and a belated response to *Brian Westby*. His final novel, *Ratman's Notebooks* (1968), the story of a loner who learns he can train rats to kill, would become his most famous, being twice filmed as *Willard* (1971 and 2003).

Gilbert married his wife Kathleen Stevenson in 1945; the two had four children, and Gilbert devoted most of his time from the 1950s onward to family life and his seed business. He died in Northern Ireland in 2010 at age 97.

Kim Newman is a London-based author and movie critic. He writes regularly for *Empire Magazine* and contributes to *The Guardian*, *The Times*, *Sight & Sound* and others. He is the author of several novels, including the *Anno Dracula* series, and has won the Bram Stoker, International Horror Guild, British Fantasy, and British Science Fiction Awards and been nominated for the Hugo and World Fantasy Awards.

BY STEPHEN GILBERT

The Landslide (1943)★

Bombardier (1944)★

Monkeyface (1948)★

The Burnaby Experiments (1952)★

Ratman's Notebooks (1968)★

★ Available from Valancourt Books

STEPHEN GILBERT

Ratman's Notebooks

With a new introduction by

KIM NEWMAN

VALANCOURT BOOKS
Richmond, Virginia
2013

Ratman's Notebooks by Stephen Gilbert
First published London: Michael Joseph, 1968
First Valancourt Books edition 2013

Published by Valancourt Books, Richmond, Virginia
Publisher & Editor: James D. Jenkins
20th Century Series Editor: Simon Stern, University of Toronto
http://www.valancourtbooks.com

Library of Congress Cataloging-in-Publication Data

Gilbert, Stephen, 1912-2010.
Ratman's Notebooks / Stephen Gilbert ; with a new introduction
by Kim Newman. – First Valancourt Books edition.
    pages cm. – (20th century series)
 ISBN 978-1-939140-60-9 *(acid-free paper)*
 1. Diaries – Fiction. 2. Revenge – Fiction. 3. Human-animal relation-
ships – Fiction. 4. Rats – Fiction. 5. Psychological fiction. 6. Suspense
fiction. I. Title.
 PR6013.I3363R38 2013
 823'.912–dc23
                                   2013024674

Cover by M.S. Corley
Set in Dante MT 11/13.2

INTRODUCTION

STEPHEN GILBERT (1912-2010) published four novels between 1943 and 1952, then busied himself with other interests for the rest of his life. He was active in his family's tea and seed shipping business, a volunteer for the Samaritans and a founder of the Northern Irish branch of the Campaign for Nuclear Disarmament. But he made an isolated return to fiction with this, his final novel, published in 1968.

Ratman's Notebooks is so unlike Gilbert's earlier work there was once some confusion about whether he was indeed the Stephen Gilbert who had written it. The online *Encyclopedia of Science Fiction* notes the book 'has erroneously been ascribed to Northern Ireland-born writer Gilbert Alexander Ralston (1912-1999), using "Stephen Gilbert" as a pseudonym. Ralston did write under his own name the screenplay for *Willard* (1971), the film of the novel (he later wrote several Westerns, all under his own name; he lived in America for many years, and was active in the film industry). The two writers may have been confused because of *Willard*, and perhaps because Ralston also seems to have been born in County Down, Northern Ireland, in 1912.'

Gilbert's earlier novels were admired by a select few (including E. M. Forster, who called his 1943 debut *The Landslide* 'an original and graceful work') but scarcely troubled the best-seller lists or paperback racks. *The Burnaby Experiments* (1952), also republished by Valancourt, is a roman à clef about Gilbert's friendship with the older author Forrest Reid, and touches on psychic powers (a theme which is developed here). However, *Ratman's Notebooks* had the good fortune to benefit from a film rights deal . . . furthermore, Daniel Mann's film adaptation, which calls Gilbert's unnamed ratman 'Willard Stiles', was a major commercial success, which means paperback editions bearing the film's title were widely available when I was a schoolboy. I first read it when I was too young to get into cinemas showing X certificate movies.

For some reason, *Willard* is hard to see these days—even when it was remade in 2003, no DVD special edition of the first film appeared. Nevertheless, it gave rise to a sequel, *Ben* (1972), remembered for Michael Jackson's hideous theme song, and lingered long enough in the memory and the box office record books to earn that remake. It's certain that the film, a good enough adaptation though it shifts the action to California, boosted the profile of the book enough to make it a paperback best-seller . . .

. . . and, because of that, horror became a mainstream publishing genre.

To backtrack, throughout the 1960s, the thin 'horror' section of W. H. Smith's contained only the annual volumes of Herbert Van Thal's *The Pan Book of Horror Stories* and Dennis Wheatley's black magic thrillers, with the occasional Penguin M.R. James reissue slipped in. A few stray best-sellers—Ira Levin's *Rosemary's Baby*, William Peter Blatty's *The Exorcist*—raised the profile of the category, but no author would consider a *career* as a horror writer. Even Robert Bloch, a *Weird Tales* veteran boosted when Alfred Hitchcock filmed his *Psycho*, stayed in the game by categorising himself as a mystery writer.

That all changed with two books first published in 1974, James Herbert's *The Rats* and Stephen King's *Carrie*. The British Herbert and the American King didn't just detour into the supernatural and horrific, as Levin and Blatty did, but stuck around, following their first novels with similar, more ambitious horror visions. King's books were filmed—so were some of Herbert's, though few noticed—and the horror section swelled, with writers like Peter Straub, F. Paul Wilson, Robert McCammon, V. C. Andrews, Anne Rice and Clive Barker. In the 1970s and '80s, there was a publishing horror boom.

And it started with *Ratman's Notebooks / Willard*.

The success of book and films made rampaging vermin a major horror theme of the 1970s and '80s, as shown in creepy-crawly movies like *Frogs*, *Squirm*, *Kingdom of the Spiders* and *Phase IV* and books like Guy N. Smith's *Crabs* novels and Shaun Hutson's *Slugs* sagas. Herbert's specific inspiration for writing *The Rats* was his East End childhood and a speech from Renfield in the 1931 film of *Dracula*, but you can bet New English Library's inspiration for publishing *The Rats* was the success of Gilbert's novel. A few other super-clever 'rat' stories in the '70s play variations on the theme—TV episodes like 'Tomorrow, the Rat' from *Doom Watch* and 'During Barty's Party' from *Nigel Kneale's Beasts*.

The influence of *Ratman's Notebooks* on *Carrie* isn't quite so blatant, but they are both entries in the sub-genre of 'turning worm' revenge fantasy (*The Count of Monte Cristo* is an ur-text). A put-upon central character suffers various slights but discovers a special ability which enables him or her to punish their tormentors, usually going power-mad and visiting terror upon the innocent as well as the guilty before being destroyed by what they've unleashed. In *Ratman's Notebooks*, it's intelligent rats . . . in *Carrie*, it's psychic powers, but the story archetype is the same for both. A few imitative films underline the link by combining the two premises: *Kiss of the Tarantula* (1976) and *Jennifer* (1978)* have Carrie-like adolescent female outcasts psychically bonding with vermin (spiders and snakes) they sic on their enemies. *Willard* even set the fashion followed by *Carrie* for naming horror movies after bland-sounding protagonists . . . which explains the terror track records of Patrick, Ruby, Stanley, Julia and others.

Indeed, by putting the terror-by-animal sub-genre of horror on the map (previously, only Daphne du Maurier's 'The Birds', filmed by Hitchcock, really fit the bill), *Ratman's Notebooks* and *Willard* cleared shelf-space for the book and film of *Jaws*, another lasting publishing and movie phenomenon.

Even beyond its little-noticed but paramount position in the mushroom growth of horror as a publishing category, *Ratman's Notebooks* is a good little novel, certainly stronger than early Herbert and better even than early King. The unnamed narrator's voice prefigures the alienated outcasts of Iain Banks's *The Wasp Factory* or Ramsey Campbell's *The Face That Must Die*. The details of his everyday miseries and growing kinship with the brilliantly characterised rats Socrates and Ben (the Martin Luther King and Malcolm X of rodentkind) are touching as well as amusing and eventually terrifying.

KIM NEWMAN

June 18, 2013

* A favourite piece of pest movie trivia—Bruce Davison, who played Willard, is married to Lisa Pelikan, who played Jennifer.

RATMAN'S NOTEBOOKS

Note

The manuscript of the journal printed on the following pages came into my hands in slightly peculiar circumstances. I was in Edinburgh on business. With me was Ralph Preston our solicitor. Ralph was staying with friends at Corstorphine and very kindly asked me to a party at their house. I had never been to this house before and didn't know any of the family.

After a while I found myself chatting with a rather shy, middle-aged man, who, I thought was my host. Suddenly he rushed off and came back with these notebooks. 'Read those,' he said, 'and see if you'd like to publish them.'

I tried to explain that I wasn't a publisher, and had no influence with publishers, but he wouldn't listen to me. 'You could get them published very well if you liked,' he insisted. And then, 'At least it wouldn't do you any harm to have a look at them.' By this time he was beginning to sound angry.

So I took the books, sat down in a corner, and began to read. I found them easy to read. The handwriting is small, neat and extremely legible. Though the entries are undated there is a space between each, indicating where one day ends and another begins. In places there seem to be considerable gaps in time.

After I had been reading for about an hour I noticed that the party was breaking up. I looked about for the person who had handed me the notebooks, but he wasn't there, and to this day I have been unable to find out any more about him. I don't think he can have been Ratman himself, but he may be the author of the note, written on a loose sheet of paper, which I found stuck between the pages of the last notebook.

My host turned out to be someone quite different from my shy, middle-aged friend. He has been very kind and helpful. But he hasn't been able to bring me any nearer to a solution of the mystery.

Mother says there are rats in the rockery.

'You'll have to do something about them,' she says, 'or they'll over-run the whole place.'

It's all very well *her* talking. I'm at business all day. I don't know what she thinks *I* can do about it. I'm afraid of rats. I don't mind admitting it. What was she doing up there anyhow? She's hardly been in the back garden since Father died. It annoys her to see how neglected it's got.

Saturday afternoon, so I thought I'd better investigate.

The rockery is at the very top of the garden. When Father was alive it was a sort of show place—very pretty, rare flowers. All that sort of thing. He used to bring along his gardening friends to show it them. There was a pool in the centre of the rockery, and he meant to put a fountain in the centre of the pool. He was working at it shortly before he died. In those days we kept a full-time gardener. But Father always looked after the rockery himself.

I hadn't been in the back garden for ages. The state of it quite shocked me. Not that I'll do anything. I'm only surprised Mother got as far as the rockery. There are brambles right across the path. In one place there's even a tree, quite a sizeable tree, growing out of the very middle of the path. It just shows. Mother's as tough as old nails really, or can be when she chooses.

After Father died we couldn't afford a gardener. I suppose we should have sold the house and moved somewhere smaller, but neither Mother nor I liked the idea. Mother wrote to Uncle in Canada and told him how badly-off we were. Uncle's a bachelor, and supposed to have money. But he didn't even reply. So we paid off the gardener and stayed on, hoping for better times. Uncle can't last forever. I keep the front garden looking fairly decent. The back's gone wild.

For the first few summers it was rather attractive that way, with the flowers fighting it out among themselves and rambler roses sprawling all over the place. In winter it got a horrible derelict look and I didn't go there much. After four years or so most of the flowers had gone, even in summer, though there were still a good many roses of one kind or another and various flowering shrubs.

I think it must have been about the third year after Father's death, one very wet night, that the pool in the rockery overflowed. The water ran down the whole length of the garden and under the back door into the yard of the house. Fortunately there's a drain in the middle of the yard and the water got away without doing much damage. I stayed at home next morning to clear up. I found the outlet of the pool had got blocked with dead leaves and rubbish. I cleared it easily enough, but I didn't want more trouble. So I cut off the water and let the pool run dry.

It was after eleven when I arrived at the office, and Mr. Jones gave off at me for being late. I tried to explain what had happened, but he just said, 'Remember you're only an ordinary employee here.' I've remembered it ever since, though I'm quite sure most of the ordinary employees would have got away with it without a word. He gets at me because he doesn't like remembering that Father was once his boss and that he started as little more than a working man. Now he's sole proprietor.

That was seven years ago, the pool overflowing and me getting into a row with Mr. Jones. Things haven't improved any at the office in the meantime, but I do my job as well as I can and try not to annoy him.

I didn't expect to see any rats straight off, and I didn't. I had brought an old waterproof with me. I spread this out on the long grass and lay down to watch. The sun was shining. I like this time of year, half-spring, half-summer. I'd just had my lunch. I felt warm, comfortable and a bit drowsy. I let myself fall asleep. After all I had the whole week-end before me. It didn't matter which particular moment I watched the rats. They would either appear or not appear.

I don't think I slept very long. Maybe half-an-hour. Maybe only five minutes. It doesn't matter. When I awoke they were there—a father rat, a mother rat, and a whole family of young ones. At least that's what I suppose. I don't really know which was the father and which the mother, but there were two big rats and about eleven little ones. My first feeling was a mixture of fear and disgust. What if the whole place was alive with them and I should suddenly find another family running over me? Perhaps they would attack me. I have heard that a cornered rat will fight. I have heard of babies being bitten by rats. I didn't feel safe. I waited for a moment or two thinking what I should do. Then I stood up suddenly, meaning to run at full speed down to the house. But the moment I was on my feet I felt more sure of myself. I decided not to run, till I should see what the rats would do.

The rats stopped playing. The two big ones immediately, the little ones a few seconds later. For a quarter of a minute or so everything froze, me standing like a statue, the two big rats watching me, the eleven little rats snuggled against stones or plants trying to make themselves invisible. Then one of the adults must have given some order. All the little ones scurried away under the big juniper bush, which grows in sort of layers close to the ground. The big ones followed. A few seconds later there wasn't a sign of any of them. I was still rather frightened. I tip-toed over and peered under the juniper bush. I couldn't see anything, but in the ground round about there are several holes which I'm sure must be rat-holes. There must be a whole colony of them. I wondered what we should do.

I went back to the house. I'd the front grass to cut, and if I'd any time afterwards I meant to do a bit of hoeing at the weeds in the drive. I keep the lawnmower in the W.C. in the yard. Mother doesn't like it there. She'd like everything to be the way it was when Father was alive. But as there's no maid now to use that W.C. I don't see any harm in keeping the tools there. It's much handier than having to run up to the old tool-shed at the top of the garden every time you want anything.

Mother saw me the moment I came into the yard. I think she must have been on the look-out for me. I didn't want to talk, but she rapped on the kitchen window and I had to go in and speak to her. She wears a diamond engagement ring, a gold wedding ring, and another ring with emeralds in it, so that when she raps on the window it is a very peremptory noise which I can't pretend not to hear.

'I wish you wouldn't keep the mower in that place,' she started off.

I said nothing. It's the only way with her. Sometimes she'll go on for quite a long time and if I talk back I find myself being argued into promising things. Then she gets at me later for not keeping my promise. So it's best to say nothing. This time she didn't go on about the lawnmower because she wanted something else. 'Did you do anything about the rats?'

'No. What could *I* do?'

'I'm sure your father would have done something. Did you even go and look at them?'

'Yes. I've been watching them.'

'Did you see them then?'

'Yes I saw them.'

'They're all over the place.'

'I don't think so. I think there's only one family of them, and they're just about the rockery so far as I could see.'

'Yes, but they grow up in no time at all and they breed very fast. If you don't do something about it they'll be over the whole place.'

'I don't know what I *can* do.'

'You'll have to do something.'

I nearly said I would think about it while I was cutting the grass, but I stopped myself in time. That would have been a promise to do something as soon as the grass was cut. I just said, 'I'm going to cut the grass.'

I managed to keep out of her way for the rest of the afternoon, but at tea-time she started again about the rats. 'I'm sure your father would have known what to do.'

'Father would probably have got a professional rat-catcher.'

'Well why don't you get a professional rat-catcher?'

'A rat-catcher'd cost money.'

In our family, even before Father died, you could stop nearly any suggestion by saying it would cost money. We never had money to spare, and now of course it's even worse.

Mother kept quiet for quite a while, and her next remark was on what seemed to be a different subject. 'I think it's ridiculous that they haven't made you a director.'

'I don't see why they should,' I mumbled sulkily. I know very well that I'm never going to be a success in business, and I didn't want to talk about it.

'Well your father was head of the firm. That should surely mean something.'

'It means I don't get the sack.'

'Nonsense. They simply make use of you. They know very well that you're trustworthy. They wouldn't get anyone else they could trust with the money for anything like what they pay you.'

'I'm sure they could get someone else if they wanted.'

'Then you should have a better job.'

This sort of talk makes me feel embarrassed and ashamed of myself. So I didn't answer. Presently she got back to the rats. 'I could pour boiling water down the rat-holes and when they came up you could kill them with a stick. You can break their backs very easily, I believe.'

For a moment this idea thoroughly scared me. I didn't want any cornered rats jumping up and tearing out *my* throat. Then I saw it wouldn't work. 'If you'd enough water you might drown them,' I suggested, 'but boiling water's just going to run away into the ground.'

'Then you could get a hose and let it run into one of the holes. You'd block the others. Any that tried to come up you'd kill with your stick.'

'It wouldn't work. They've far too many holes. You'd never find them all.'

'You don't want to do anything at all,' she retorted. 'You're bone-lazy. That's the trouble. You're probably lazy in business too, and that's why you don't get on.'

'Very probably,' I agreed. 'I wonder which side of the family I get that from.'

In spite of all this, the talk of drowning the rats gave me an idea, and later in the evening, when we were on speaking terms again, I mentioned it to her. 'You know the pool in the rockery.'

'I thought it had been drained.'

'So it was, but if we could entice the rats in there and then fill it with water, they'd drown all right.'

This idea pleased her. 'I knew you'd think of something if I kept at you. All you need is a little prodding. What you want's a wife to keep after you the whole time. I'm getting too old for it. It would help you in business too.'

Of course she knows very well that I can't afford to get married, even if I wanted to. And if she saw any chance of it she'd fight tooth and nail to stop me.

I never work in the garden on Sundays. Mother wouldn't approve. I started on the pool this evening, Monday, immediately after tea. It's going to be a much bigger job than I thought, but it's the sort of job I can enjoy. I don't mean actually drowning the rats—probably I shan't look at that—but all the preparations. It's turning out to be a really dirty job, and there's something about dirty jobs, once you get stuck into them.

I started off with a shovel and wheel-barrow. The pool is silted up with a sort of black sludge, a mixture of earth and water, half-rotten leaves and broken twigs. I can't simply shovel it out. It's full of growing things, plants of all kinds, grass and young trees. The roots are tangled together. Each time I thought I'd got a shovelful whatever was on the shovel was dragged off before I could pitch it into the barrow. I tried cutting through the roots with a spade, but that wasn't much good either. I was afraid to use it too energetically for fear of breaking the concrete. I don't think it's very thick. If I cracked it the water would drain away and the rats wouldn't get drowned. So I mucked in and dragged out the growing stuff with my hands. I'll have more use for the shovel and spade later, when all the roots are gone and there's only mud to clear.

I got into the house tonight at half-past ten. I was black from head to toe. Mother hardly knew me. I had to have a bath straight away.

Well the first part's nearly done. I've got the pool itself more or less the way it was when Father left it. It's about twelve feet across and the island in the centre is about three feet. The island is made of old paving stones piled on top of each other. I'll take off the top two layers, so that the island will be below the level of the edge of the pool. It's essential that the island should become completely submerged when I let the water in.

The next thing is to clear the channel which brings the water from the old mill-pond in the field at the back. This needn't be a thorough job. I'll just have to make sure the water flows once the sluice-gate is opened.

I could almost find it in my heart to do the whole thing properly. Seeing it like this reminds me of it at its best. It really *was* quite attractive. All I'd have to do would be to clear the little path round the pool, and of course weed the rockery. . . . I suppose I'd have to put in fresh plants to take the place of the ones that have disappeared, and then go on weeding it once a week or so—every night more likely. Once a week would never keep up with it seeing I keep the front as well.

Mother'd be delighted, but I shan't do it. I hate any job I must do again and again. I hate cutting the grass and hoeing endlessly at the weeds in the drive. I'd let everything go completely if it wasn't for Mother. She keeps at me. It's not as if she ever did a stroke in the garden herself. She says she wears her fingers to the bone looking after the house, but I never see much sign of it.

Tomorrow'll be Saturday again and everything is ready for the execution. The pool is empty and dry. All that is now necessary is to ensure the attendance of the victims. There'd be no sense in trying anything too soon. I'll throw a few scraps into the bottom of the pool tomorrow afternoon and see if they get taken.

Another week's gone by and the whole scheme is working out much better than I expected, that is to say than I expected recently. At first I hardly thought out any details.

I threw in some scraps on Saturday afternoon. The rats can't even have seen them. They were still there on Sunday morning. On Sunday afternoon some sparrows found them. On Sunday evening I put in more. By Monday evening they were all gone, but I wasn't sure if it was rats or sparrows. So I got lumps of bread from the house, threw them in, and waited. After about a minute I saw Ma Rat looking out at me from under the edge of the juniper bush, or whatever it is. We watched each other. Soon I got tired and sat down. Ma Rat went on watching me. After another five minutes or so she moved slowly over to the empty pool and peered down at the lumps of bread lying on the bottom. Then I noticed the young rats. They appeared first at the edge of the bush. Then one by one, in short rushes, a yard or so at a time, they lined up beside their mother. They all peered down at the bread in the pool.

Suddenly one of the young ones half-jumped half-scrambled down the side of the pool. At the bottom he paused and looked round cautiously. Ma looked round too. Next minute they were all at the bread. Ma was the last. She jumped down very awkwardly and heavily. It looks as if she were in the family-way again. No sign of Father Rat. I wonder has he deserted.

Well everything *is* ready now. I've got the top two layers of slabs off the island, which I forgot about before. I've got the rats quite into the habit of feeding in the pool, or on the island to be exact. I still put a few scraps on the bottom of the pool to attract them in the first place, and make the whole thing look casual. As if I was dumping rubbish there. But most of the food goes on the island. They'll all be congregated on the island, eating, and won't notice the water flowing in till it's too late. At least that's the idea. They'll be quite undisturbed. Even *I* shan't be there to watch—at the beginning. Of course I'll be there before the end—in time to see them drown. It'll be horrid, but I won't be able to resist.

Everything worked perfectly. Immediately after tea I went up the garden with a big bowl of scraps. True to tradition the last meal of the condemned had to be good, nothing spared. Mother would have liked to come and watch, but she's not been well the last day or two. She felt the walk up the garden might be too much for her. We were both excited. I promised to run down to the house and tell her immediately the deed was done.

I threw the scraps on the island. Some of them dropped off into the bottom of the pool, and one bit of bacon rind dangled over the edge of the island. I paused just a moment to make sure the rats had spotted that it was 'Grub up', as I believe they say in the army. Then I hurried away to open the sluice-gate. The pond the water comes from is about seventy-five yards from the pool. The sluice-gate is wooden and runs in grooves. There is a long ratchet coming up from the gate. The teeth of the ratchet fit into a cog on a winch. I had the cog and ratchet well greased. I turned the winch handle and the sluice-gate—it's only about a foot wide—rose slowly. In spite of the grease the mechanism creaked a bit. It hasn't been used for years. At first the water seemed reluctant to leave the pond. The bottom of the ditch isn't deep enough to make the water rush out quickly. Even a bit of ragged robin growing across the ditch held it back for a moment as if it had been a dam. Then it trickled through and gradually the flow became a little faster, more decided. . . . Nothing much, but enough—provided it was getting through into the pool.

I ran back to the stile which leads from the garden to the field. I stood on the top step. I could see the pool, but I wasn't close enough to make out what was happening. I got off the stile and tip-toed a bit closer.

The water was flowing very gently into the pool. All the rats except one were on top of the island. This one was just below the others on the floor of the pool. He was reaching up for the piece of bacon rind I had noticed before, hanging over the edge. He got it and almost at the same moment felt a trickle of water against his tail. He twitched his tail in and hopped up a little on to the lower stones of the island. He wasn't a bit perturbed. He was able to reach more food from his new position. He started to eat a bit of crust, holding it up in the air between his hands. They were all eating away, unconscious of the rising water. They'd never had a feast like it. Still no sign of Father Rat. I wondered what had happened to him. I didn't like to think of him escaping. The rat who'd got his tail wet moved a little higher up the shore of the island.

All the rats went on eating. Slowly the water rose. Two inches deep. If they tried they could still walk through it and jump up on to the edge of the pool. I wondered would they, if they noticed, but they didn't notice. Three inches, four. . . . The rat on the shore hopped up a little further before the advancing tide. Five inches, six inches. . . .

The water was at least nine inches deep before Ma Rat noticed anything. Even then she didn't get excited. She raised her head, looked round, sniffed, twitched her whiskers. 'It's too late now, Ma. It's no good swimming for it. The edges of the pool are smooth concrete. You can scrabble away, but you won't be able to get a foothold and scramble out. Besides if any of you look like succeeding I can knock you back with my stick. I've brought a stick out with me specially for the purpose.' I didn't say this out loud. I thought it.

Ma Rat went to the edge of the island and peered down. It's steep there, a sort of miniature cliff edge. No. More like a quay wall. Ma Rat watched the water lapping against the quay wall. She was puzzled. She didn't know she was living at the sea-side. She started on a tour of the coast. On the way she met her gormless son still peacefully taking his supper among the rocks on the lower part of the shore. She made an angry snap at him with her teeth. She thought he should have noticed something. I don't know if she actually nipped him or not, but he let out a little squeal of dismay. This upset the whole family. They all started scurrying backwards and forwards, peering at the water from every side of the island in turn. They seemed to think there must be one side where there wasn't any water.

I came nearer. I didn't mind the rats seeing me now. I contemplated the scene. How smoothly the water rose, creeping up the edge of the pool, hardly a ripple anywhere, slow, grey, inevitable.

At first the rats didn't seem to notice me. They rushed to and fro uttering their little squeals of excitement. I don't think they realised yet what was happening to them. Ma didn't squeal. *She* knew what was happening. At least she realised the water was rising, that the island was going to be submerged. That was the moment I was waiting for. Would they try to swim for it? Or would they wait till the water was actually lapping over them and swim then?

Ma stared out over the water. Trying to make up her mind, I suppose. Should she plunge in and swim for the bank, or should she just wait? I thought all rats could swim. But maybe they don't all *know* they can. Maybe Ma never had to swim before. I wonder what the water looked like to her. I don't know how well rats can see. Perhaps they can't see very far. Perhaps the edge of the pool seemed a long way away.

Suddenly she caught sight of me. I don't know how I knew that she'd seen me, but I did. She peered up at me. I stood there on a little mound of the rockery, a huge god-like figure, unmoving, terrible. . . .

The young rats were really scared at last. They were all milling round the island in a panic, screaming, calling on their mother to save them. I'd never heard a rat scream before. Ten of them doing it at once made an appalling row. Ma herself didn't utter a sound.

I didn't see her simply as a rat any more. I saw her as a mother worrying about her children.

She stared at me very fixedly. She'd made up her mind what to do. She got into a position. . . . I don't know what to call it. Rats don't exactly kneel. It was a position of supplication. She clasped her hands together. She prayed to me. 'Please save my children. It doesn't matter about me. Let me drown if you like, but please spare my children.'

At first I did nothing. I contemplated her quite stonily. They were all crowded together. There wasn't much island left. Soon they'd start pushing each other off.

Something happened to me. My stoniness melted. I was filled with compassion. For a moment I didn't know what to do. Too late to run and lower the sluice-gate. By the time I got the flow stopped the water would be over their heads. I noticed a heavy plank lying at the side of the pool. I had used it as a ramp for the wheelbarrow when I was clearing the rubbish out of the pool. Now I picked it up and edged it across the water till the far end rested on the stones of the island. It made a bridge from the island to the mainland. Ma Rat didn't waste an instant. She hopped on and came scurrying across with the whole family streaming after her. None of this 'After you, Clarence.' Leadership. That's how she brings up her family. As she passed me she gave a kind of little bow. I don't know what else to call it. She led her family over to the juniper bush. She put her head between her front paws and bowed down to me. It was a sort of prayer of gratitude. She was acknowledging that I had saved her family.

I'm puzzled. Does she know it was I who planned the destruction of herself and her family? I don't suppose so. Probably she thinks I just happened along in time to save them. But I'm not sure. At any rate I feel there is now a definite relationship established between me and Ma Rat. I believe she regards me as a kind of god.

I went back to the house. 'Well?' Mother asked. 'How did you get on?'

'I got the job done.'

'All of them?'

'All except the old father. I haven't seen him for some time.

Maybe he's had an accident, or perhaps he's got another wife some-where else.'

'I shouldn't be a bit surprised,' Mother said. She likes to be reminded of the wickedness of the world, even if it's only the Rat world. 'Did none of them try to swim to the edge and climb out?'

'Only one. I knocked it back with a stick. It went on swimming round and round for quite a long time. It's funny. Some of them gave up quite soon and others went on swimming and swimming till I thought they were never going to drown.'

'But they all did in the end?'

'Yes. I think the longest must have been about twenty minutes.'

It's funny the pleasure it gave me telling these lies to Mother. They were so absolutely deliberate. I relished them.

But Mother's a dangerous person to lie to. You need to be very careful. 'Did the bodies sink or float?' she enquired.

I didn't hesitate a moment. 'Oh they sank. That's how I knew they were drowned.'

'I didn't know whether they'd sink or not. I suppose the bodies are all lying on the bottom of the pool.'

'They are at present.'

'I expect they'll rise to the top in about ten days or so when the gas forms inside them.'

'Oh I'll drain the pond again and clear them away before that happens.'

She didn't say anything more, but suddenly I knew that tomor-row, when I was safely away at business, she'd be up at the pool to contemplate the corpses—and nothing would she see.

I waited for a little and then got up quietly and went out of the room. I went back up to the pool. The island was completely covered now, but the water wasn't rising any more. It was getting away by the overflow which took it to the stream in the glen at the far side of our house.

I went into the field and lowered the sluice-gate so that the water stopped flowing into the channel that led to the pool. Then I went back to the garden and opened the stop-cock below the pool so that all the water drained out. After that I footered about for a bit to put in time. It was dark when I got back to the house.

'Where have you been all this time?' Mother demanded immediately.

'Oh I thought I'd better finish the job when I was at it. I drained the pool again and cleared out the bodies.'

'What did you do with them?'

'Oh I disposed of them. You didn't want to see them, did you?'

'No of course not.' But she was lying just as much as I was.

Mother keeps asking me what I've been doing. I tell her I've been working in the garden. It's true in a way, though she mightn't call it work. At the moment she doesn't feel like coming out on a tour of inspection. The path at the back is too steep. If she does manage it some day I don't know what I'm going to tell her. She's going to have difficulty finding evidence of my work.

What I'm doing, or trying to do, is to make Ma Rat understand things I say to her. So far my success has been nil. She's not stupid by any means. I've taught her one or two things. I've got a big box, lined with sheet metal, where I keep food for her. At first she was frightened of it, in case it might be some kind of trap, I suppose. There's a door in one side of it which she can open and close herself. It was easy enough to teach her how to open it, but for a long time she wouldn't close it. I had to get it into her head that if she didn't close it the food would be stolen. At first I would close it for her. Then I would leave it open the odd time. If it had been left open there'd be no food next time. I had to hold her hands to show her how to shut it. She didn't like it much at first, but now she trusts me completely—and of course I'm not afraid of *her* any more. The trouble about speech is that she doesn't realise it *is* speech. She knows that I make various vocal noises, just as I know that she makes vocal noises. But I can't make sense out of any of her utterances. I don't think there's sense in them. She signifies fear by screaming—they all do—pleasure perhaps by little grunts, though I'm not sure of this. But it's not intended to convey any message. It hasn't occurred to them to use sound as a means of communication. Therefore it doesn't occur to her that the sounds I make have any particular significance, unless they're specially loud. If I shout she stops whatever she is doing and looks at me. So I suppose she is learning that I use sound as a means of attracting attention.

The family I saved from drowning has all disappeared. The new family has been born—I know that by the shape of her, though I haven't seen any of them yet. I don't even see her husband. This friendship is a personal thing between her and me.

I think perhaps I am going to succeed. About a month ago I made two boxes. They're both more or less the same, though not identical. They're very rough. I'm not a carpenter by any standards. The boxes have lids with bits of an old strap acting as hinges. The lids aren't fastened in any way. Every night I've been putting the food I bring into one or other of these boxes. Every night I point to one box and say, 'Food.' For the last three nights she's gone straight to the box with the food in it.

  I'll go on doing this for another week without any change. After that I'll start pointing to each of the boxes in turn. As I point to one I shall say, 'Food.' When I point to the other I shall say, 'Empty.'

I don't know how long I've been at the new system now, probably nearly two months. At last I think I may be getting somewhere. At first I couldn't tell if she was paying any attention to what I said, or not. Once she went to the right box three nights running. The following four nights she went to the wrong one. What makes me think she has begun to listen is that for the past week or so I've noticed her watching my face, waiting for me to speak, before she goes to either box. Of course she might be lip-reading. That would be a strange thing, but perhaps not unlikely. I make a great difference in the way I pronounce the two words. I say, 'Emmmm teeee' in a harsh unattractive voice. But when I say, 'Food,' it's in a soft caressing tone, 'Foooooood.'

Certainly it's working, but where do I go from here? Incidentally Ma's at her third family since I first got to know her.

Very strange. Ma appears to have had a family of one, or else something's happened to the others. Stranger still she brought this one along this evening and introduced him. It was more than an introduction. You would almost have thought she was giving him to me.

There is something about him that is odd. I can't help feeling that he is human. He is not frightened of me at all. When Ma brought him along he looked at me, shyly perhaps, but with no sign of fear. He looked at me as a friendly and intelligent boy might look at a new tutor, who he has been told is very kind. Of course I don't really know that he is a male. I am convinced he is—on absolutely no evidence. I have no idea how you tell the difference between male and female rats.

I have called him Socrates. I thought of Samuel, by a peculiar sort of association of ideas, but Socrates is better. He looks so wise.

Socrates I would say is less than half-grown, that is to say he is less than half the size of Ma. I don't know what age that would make him, but judging by the time since the last family departed I don't think he can be more than six weeks old. He is handsome. The fur on his back is dark brown and glossy. His paws and chest and all his underpart are white. He is very clean. His eyes seem a little larger than those of the other rats I have seen, and seem to have a sort of gleam of intelligence. This may be my imagination. I'm not sure if eyes are capable of expression. His ears move all the time. When he is looking at me and listening to me his whole expression is alert and bright. At present his tail is pinkish and much thinner than his mother's. I don't find it repulsive looking. Perhaps it will get fat and scaly when he grows up.

He knows his name already. It only took him about fifteen minutes to learn it and funnily enough Ma learned her name at the same time. I just call her, 'Ma.'

Socrates has already learned to pick out the full and the empty box. This all in one evening. I mean it's only this evening that I saw him for the first time. But I changed my method a little. Instead of saying, 'Fooood. . . . Emmm-teee,' I changed to 'Fooood,' and 'No fooood.' I intend to go on to lots of other things in the same way—'Water,' and 'No water' and so on.

Ma didn't appear tonight. Only Socrates. Ma is about due for another family. She seems to have one about every six weeks. What happens to them all I can't imagine.

Socrates learns extraordinarily quickly. First thing tonight I tried him to see if he remembered 'Food' and 'No Food.' It was quite clear that he did. I tried him several times, changing the food from one box to another without letting him see. Every time he went to the box I told him the food was in. Next I tried to teach him the word 'Box.' I touched one box after the other and said, 'Boxes.' I think he understands, but it's impossible to know. If he were a child, he would repeat the words after me, but I can't expect that. All I'm trying to do is to make him understand what I say, not to make him talk back at me. I ought to be able to think out some system.

I suppose I'm stupid, but I can't really think out any system. I just keep talking all the time I'm with him. I'm sure some of it sticks in his brain, but I don't know how much. I say, 'I, Me, Man,' and point at myself. I say, 'You, Rat,' and point at him.

I got a trowel from the tool shed and dug a small hole near the pool in the rockery. I said, 'I dig hole. Me dig hole. Man dig hole. I, me, man dig hole.' That was while I was digging. When I had finished I pointed to the hole and said several times, 'Hole, hole. Man made hole.'

Socrates looked at me and he looked at the hole. He seemed to understand. Suddenly I had an inspiration. 'Rat-hole,' I said. Sure enough he scampered away to the hole under the juniper bush. 'Man-hole,' I called after him and he came scurrying back to the hole I had made. Well that proved that he did understand and that he learns extraordinarily quickly, but of course I've taught him one word wrongly. I'll have to try to teach him what a man-hole really is.

Socrates' tail isn't pink any more. It's covered with fine hairs, like a sort of brown fuzz.

Tonight I set off with Socrates in my pocket to find a man-hole. There are really quite a lot of man-holes, but they all seem to be in the middle of roads. Eventually I got one in what I thought was a quiet place and put Socrates down on it so that he could sniff round and see what it was. The next thing I knew there was a screaming of brakes and here was a car coming straight at us. I dived down, grabbed Socrates and shoved him under my jacket. But I hadn't time to jump for the side of the road before the car skidded past sideways making a dreadful noise. I got an awful fright and felt very cross.

But what do you think happened? The car stopped facing into the ditch, sideways on to the road, but no harm done. The chap jumped out almost before it had stopped and came tearing over to me, as if there wasn't a moment to lose. I thought he was going to apologise for nearly running me down. But not a bit of him. 'What the hell do you think you're doing?' he said.

'I wasn't doing anything,' I told him.

'Well for God's sake go and do it somewhere else. You're damned lucky I didn't kill you.'

'You were driving far too fast,' I retorted. 'You ought to be more careful.'

He was going to hit me. I don't think I'm a coward, though I certainly would never want to get into a fight if I could help it. But I simply couldn't fight at that moment. I still had Socrates clasped under my jacket. I hadn't had time to put him into my pocket. At the first blow the man might easily have hit him, perhaps even killed him. And I didn't dare to put him down. The man would then have *tried* to kill him. So I just turned round and ran away as hard as I could belt.

After I'd got about fifty yards I realised he wasn't coming after me. I turned to see what he was doing. 'You're yeller,' he shouted.

'Yeller yourself,' I shouted back. 'Why haven't you got your L-plates up?'

He nearly went purple at that. 'You wait,' he roared. 'I'll get you yet.'

He rushed back towards the car, where two or three of his pals had got out and were standing around. Obviously he intended to come after me in the car, and his pals with him. So I nipped off across a field, and got home quickly by the back way before he had time to see where I was going. I hope all the same I don't meet him somewhere else.

The fur on Socrates' tail has got quite thick.

I had an unpleasant time in the office today. My salary has been the same ever since before Father died. Ten years and not a single rise. Mother's been at me time after time to go and see Jones and, as she calls it, 'Demand my rights.' She's got an idea that because Father once owned the place some sort of hereditary vested interest must have descended to me. She quite ignores the fact that we had to sell out every share Father possessed to Jones. It wasn't just Jones himself of course. He hadn't much money at that time. He managed to get someone to back him. Mother feels we sold out for too little. In a way she's right. But the business was doing badly for several years before Father's death, and I could never have made a go of it. I know I'm not a businessman, and never will be. I suppose Mother knows too, but every now and then she tries to pump what she calls 'Ambition' into me. 'Ambition!' As if I ever wanted to be a person like Jones.

At any rate she got me to promise to see Jones and ask for a rise. 'If you can't open your mouth and ask for a rise, you're never going to get anywhere,' she said, probably truly. Not that I really want to get anywhere that I know of. I just want to stay where I am and have people leave me alone.

I waited till after Jones had done the cheques at half-past eleven. Then I said, 'I wonder if I could speak to you in private for a minute, Mr. Jones.' I don't call him 'Sir.' After all, as Mother says, it really should be him calling me, 'Sir.'

'All right,' he said, 'but better make it snappy. I haven't much time to waste.'

That made me nervous to start with. I don't know whether he did it on purpose or not. All the staff say he's terrified of anyone asking for a rise. He's only made the place pay by cutting all the expenses to a minimum—all except his own salary. I know what that is. He's doubled it since Father died. Oh *he's* doing well enough. But all the same everyone says it really does upset him to be asked for a rise. He feels that if everyone got a rise the place would start losing money again, and then where'd he be? He's a great one for saving the pence, though you wouldn't say exactly that he lets the pounds look after themselves. When any of the staff want to speak to him in private he knows it's ten to one it's a rise they're after. He can't very well refuse to see them, but that's what he'd like to do.

I followed him into his private office. Father's office, really. I can't think of it any other way. He didn't sit down or ask me to. That would have looked as if he had time to talk. 'Well? What is it?'

'Please Mr. Jones, I was wondering if you could see your way to increase my salary.'

He interrupted me before I could get any further, shaking his head and putting on a most mournful expression. 'I'm sorry. Things have got very tight. We're having a terrible job making ends meet. We couldn't manage it at all.'

'But I haven't had a rise since Father died, and everything's getting dearer and dearer.'

Another shake of his head. 'No one knows that better than me. Costs rising the whole time. It's the Devil's own job making a profit—and besides you're getting more than any cashier we ever had before. You should be very comfortably off, living out there with your mother, unmarried, and your own house. . . .'

'I've got a position to keep up.' This was a thing Mother'd told me to say. I didn't like it very much, but I knew she'd ask me when I got home.

'What position?'

'Well, Father's son and all that.'

He sneered. 'You can't go through life being "Father's son." The sooner you get that into your head the better. And if I might give you another bit of advice when I'm at it. You should sell that house you live in. It's far too big for the two of you, and too expensive. You'd get on a lot better if you moved to somewhere smaller. Now get back to your work. You may be thankful you've *got* a job and a well paid one at that, considering all you're asked to do.'

Next moment I was in the passage again, wondering how I'd got there. I went back to my desk in the Cash Office. When I tried to write I found my hand shaking. I couldn't do anything for ten or fifteen minutes. I hate Jones.

I dreaded going home. I knew Mother'd be at me. And sure enough, as soon as we sat down to tea, she started up. Had I spoken to Jones? What had he said? Why hadn't I told him this and that? I told *her* as little as I could. Why she has to keep bludgeoning away at me I don't know. She should realise by this time that I'm never going to be any good by her standards, or anyone else's I suppose. I wish she'd accept the fact that I'm a failure and not keep probing me for details. It's not going to do any good. I am ashamed of myself, of being no more than I am. I am ashamed of what happened today with Jones. I hated telling her about it. I hate thinking about it. I hate Mother for having driven me to demand an interview with him. If she'd left me alone I'd never have said a word. Most of all I hate Jones.

As soon as we'd got the washing-up done I escaped out into the garden. 'Where are you away to now?' Mother called after me, but I pretended not to hear. It was dark. I went up the path to the tool-shed. I've an old hurricane-lamp there. I lit it and waited.

I had an overcoat on. So I wasn't cold. Not the coat I go to the office in, but an old one of Father's, which is far better quality and warmer than anything I could afford. The tool-shed is just the same as it always was. I used to like coming here on rainy days when I was a child and talking to the gardener. The funny thing is that it still has the same smell as I remember it having in those days. A smell of dry earth perhaps, and some chemical . . . ? Lime? Bone-meal? I don't know. I don't even know what bone-meal is. Ground down bones I suppose.

There I was anyhow, looking at the spades and forks hanging against the wall, a bit rusty perhaps but pretty much the way they were in old William's day, the old Pennsylvania lawnmower in the corner behind the door—and there was Socrates, peering out at me from a hole beneath the bench.

'Socrates,' I said, 'I've had a beastly day.'

He came right out and hopped up a sort of staircase I've made out of old boxes on to the bench. Of course I'd a few scraps for him in my pocket, but for a long time I just stood there stroking him, mostly with one finger. It soothed me somehow doing this. I began to feel at peace, at ease.

After a while Ma appeared with her latest family. I've taught them to understand a few things already and of course Socrates is a great help. He acts as a sort of school-teacher. They do a few tricks to order. One of them is to tear up a newspaper. I had one with me tonight, just to see them at it. I unfolded one sheet and put it on the bench. 'Tear it up,' I said.

They certainly did. You should have seen the fury of them. It made me laugh. They tore it to shreds.

'Stop!' I said, and they stopped just like that.

Then I had an idea. If they would tear up paper to command, why not other things? Why not motor-tyres, for instance? Why not Jones's motor-tyres? Of course motor-tyres are a lot tougher than paper. But if they went for the sides of the tyres where they're not so thick. . . . People who make me suffer should suffer in return.

'Where do you go to every night?' Mother asks me. 'You can't be working in the garden at this time of year. You couldn't see to work.'

Sometimes I tell her one thing. Sometimes another. 'I'm going out for a walk,' I told her one night. 'Need a bit of exercise after being stuck in the office all day.'

It was after eleven when I came back, but she had waited up for me. 'Have a nice walk?'

'Oh yes, *very* nice. It's a lovely frosty night. The sky's quite clear. It's almost as bright as day in the moonlight.'

'I didn't hear the gate creak, when you went out.'

'No. I left it open when I came back from the office.'

She can't catch me out though she's always trying. I've begun to enjoy lying to her. Sometimes I lie to her when it's not necessary.

'Your father always insisted on the gate being kept shut, to keep the dogs out. They make a mess of the lawn.'

She means they make messes on the lawn. 'They can get in whether the gate's shut or not,' I said. 'The hedge is full of holes. They can get in anywhere they like.'

'But your father had wire-netting put all round the hedge on the inside. I remember it cost quite a lot of money.'

'It's all rusted away.'

Quite often I tell her the truth. 'I've just been up at the tool-shed.' But she doesn't believe me. It might as well be another lie.

'What do you *do* up at the tool-shed?'

'I sit there.'

'You can't just sit there for two hours doing nothing.'

'Yes. I like it there.'

'It must be cold out. You'd be far better sitting with me in the house, or do you find my company unbearable?'

'No. I like sitting with you too.'

She doesn't know what to make of me. She thinks I have a girl, or a woman rather—not the sort of woman I could introduce to her. All the same she longs to meet her. I imagine she wants to pour out a denunciation of sin and bring me back repentant to the fold. She's very odd about it. I think she respects me more now she thinks I'm a sinner than she did when she looked on me as an innocent lamb.

She keeps saying it's about time I got married, but she doesn't really want me to marry. Not that there's the slightest chance. No girl would look at me twice. Not unless she was desperate. Not even then. Girls have a great nose for money. They have to have. They're like cats, prowling round to find the best place to have kittens. When Father was alive I used sometimes to notice girls running their eyes over me, but it never came to anything. I remember one of them telling me that she thought I would suit her best friend. But most of them didn't even think I was up to that standard. I don't know how they knew. Nowadays they don't even give me a second glance.

It's not that I'm not attracted to them. They'd upset my life just as much as any other man's if I didn't watch myself. If there was just the sexual act, over and done with in five minutes, I wouldn't mind. It's the preliminaries and the consequences I won't put up with. Why should I? Why be a slave? It's easy enough to let off steam when you have to.

It's strange how obedient they are. I can see that tearing up newspapers might be fun—and there's no doubt rats are playful. But fancy tearing up motor tyres with your teeth. The secret of course is that they tear very little at a time. And it's not just teeth. It's teeth and claws. The claws go like fury.

Doing Jones's tyres is going to be quite a thing. I will have to plan every detail like a military operation. Jones lives at the other end of town. The difficulty is going to be getting the rats there. I should like to take twelve as well as Socrates. Another difficulty. A thing like this should be rehearsed, time after time, till there is no possibility of mistake. I can't rehearse. Not the actual assault, and that's going to be the tricky part.

I feel I have got to be very careful. Rats are regarded as Enemies of Man. Even the sentimentalists don't protest about killing rats. They're not like the bunnies, and the sweet little hares and the foxes. The reason is that everyone's scared stiff of them. In my lifetime I've known people have more or less the same feeling about Germans and Japs. Now it's Communists and Chinese. The best rat is a dead rat. I wonder if rats could be a danger to the whole human race. They might be if there was a struggle for survival after a nuclear war. They breed so quickly they might be able to reproduce before succumbing to atomic sickness.

If I had a rehearsal it could only be by attacking the tyres of some other car. Once one car has been done everyone is going to be on the alert. There will be rat-traps in garages and all sorts of things. I have no desire to ruin any other person's tyres—only Jones's. In particular I don't want to try anything near home.

One part I have been able to rehearse. I have been getting my team accustomed to travelling about in a suitcase. Of course I put Socrates in with them to keep them in order. He will be like the trainer travelling with the team. I suppose I'm the manager.

First of all I just carried them about the garden. It was comic. I could feel them scurrying about inside the case. I had to say, 'Quiet! Keep still!' It didn't have much effect. I took them back to the shed. It's going to take a bit more training to accustom them to the idea that once they're in the case they must stay absolutely quiet and still till I let them out again. I couldn't go on the bus with a case and have all sorts of squeaks and squeals coming from inside. People would look at me, specially if I seemed to be talking to my suitcase.

I am having to change the team a bit. The best gnawers and clawers are not necessarily the most disciplined. I wouldn't know which ones to leave out if it wasn't for Socrates. When they come out of the box he snaps at the ones which have been giving trouble.

One thing has been bothering me. They have been practising on some old tyre covers that were hanging up on the walls of our garage, relics of the days when we had a car. Jones's tyres will have air in them. As soon as the rats get through to the tube there'll be a frightful hissing. Is that going to frighten the whole lot off? It doesn't matter if it frightens the ones that have got through, but I don't want it to start a general panic. I want to make sure he finds four flat tyres first thing in the morning, not just one.

I bought a packet of children's balloons. I blow them up and let the air come hissing out while the rats are at the tyres. I've also burst one or two. They're getting accustomed to all sorts of noises. Whatever happens now they just go on. That's discipline for you.

This evening I made rather a funny discovery. I said 'Goodnight' to Mother and went up to my room in the usual way. As soon as I switched on the light the bulb went. Phut!—like that. I went down to the cupboard under the stairs where we keep spare bulbs, but there were none left. I wondered for a moment and then decided to borrow the bulb from what used to be the maid's room, on the top floor at the back. It hadn't been used for years—or so I thought.

I went up, left the landing light on and the door open, but didn't at first put on the light in the room itself. Then it struck me that the arrangement of the room was rather odd. So I put on the light. There was a deck-chair with cushions on it in the window, and on a table beside the chair Father's old field glasses.

Mother has been spying on me. Well! Let her spy. It's not going to do *me* any harm, and if she catches her death of cold it's *her* look-out. I took the bulb from the box-room instead. I don't want her to know *I* know. It might only lead to a fresh crop of questions, and bogus explanations by me.

As it is I don't think she'll see anything. Even if she did notice a rat occasionally it wouldn't interest her. What she's expecting is a 'Female Form' flitting guiltily in or out of the tool-shed door. All the same I'll stick a bit of paper over the window of the tool-shed. That'll both convince her of the rightness of her suspicions, and make it less likely that she should see the rats.

I wonder how long she's been at it. Now I come to think of it I came in in rather a hurry one night about a month ago and found her on the first landing with her coat and hat on—all dressed to go out in fact. 'You're not going out?' I said. 'It's frightfully cold.'

'No, no. I'm not going out.'

'You've not *been* out?'

'No, no.' And then after a rather embarrassed pause, 'I put on my coat and hat for a little. Is there any harm in that?' Mother would never tell a direct lie, but she has no compunction about leading you to believe what isn't true. And it's wonderful what old people can get away with. I simply thought 'Poor old Mother *is* getting old *and* a bit queer.' And I wondered how long it would be before I had to get her put in one of these old people's homes. Quite a relief when the time comes. I'd just as soon have the house to myself, but I'm sure she'll fight tooth and nail to stay on here.

Today I went over to have a look at Jones's house. There is nothing very special about it. It's not as big a house as ours and it hasn't nearly as much garden, but of course it's *where* it is that matters. Jones lives in the *best* neighbourhood, in among the local tycoons. That's another way of saying he's got a lot of uncaught crooks around him. He's in his element.

Everything about the house and garden is neat, tidy and smart —just the way our place used to look when Father was alive. Not that Jones would need a gardener for all the bit of garden he has. Probably he and the wife look after it on Saturday afternoons. If so, you might say it's a credit to him. Why people want to spend their time grubbing about in gardens just to impress the neighbours I don't know.

The garage is beside the house, though not actually part of it. When I first arrived it was standing open, with the car inside. Obviously I couldn't hang about outside. Jones might have come out and seen me. So I walked past quickly close to the hedge. To begin with I had only that one glance through the gateway, because the hedge is high and too thick to be seen through. This was an advantage in a way. I didn't want him peering out of his drawing room window and seeing me. I walked quickly on up the avenue, and on into another avenue. . . . I didn't want anyone to notice me. I don't think anyone did. I was just a chap out for a walk. I came back again about an hour and a half later. It was dusk, nearly dark. The garage door was shut and bolted. Going past quickly, not appearing to look in, I couldn't make out if there was a padlock on it or not.

I didn't turn and have another look. Instead I went for another little walk and came back when it was quite dark. I was nervous and excited. I could feel my heart beating. No one to see me now. I opened one half of the gate, an iron gate, but it didn't even squeak. I stood for a little inside the gate, in the shadow, where the light from the street lamp didn't shine on me. The house looked rather bigger than in daylight, rather vague and mysterious. There was only light in one room, the drawing room, I suppose. Jones is careful with his money. No waste.

Of course I still couldn't see if there was a lock on the garage door or not. I couldn't really see the garage door at all. I stole in a little further on tip-toe. Crunch! Crunch! They must spend a fortune on gravel these people. I skipped on to the grass. That was better. I reached the garage door with hardly any more noise. I felt it with my hands. It's a wooden door with a bolt and padlock. Jones looks after his own.

Suddenly there was a shriek behind me. I nearly died on the spot. It went through me as if my bowels had suddenly been snatched out and hurled into deep freeze. It was Jones's daughter. Fortunately she didn't see my face. I was too frightened to turn round. I stood there, frozen, one hand on the lock. I'd been going to give it a good tug to see if it would come off.

After a moment during which both the girl and I stood absolutely still, she ran up to the front door shouting, 'Daddy! Come quick. There's a man trying to steal the car.'

I came to life at that and tore away as fast as I could. I wasn't sure which way to go. If I came dashing on to the main road, a lot of people might see me and be able to point me out if the whole Jones family and all the neighbours came pouring after me in full hue and cry. Instead I went away from the main road, running on my toes as fast as I could go. I knew there was a cross avenue about fifty yards away. I turned into this and stopped running. I sauntered along slowly as if I hadn't a care in the world.

I took the next turn to the right and came back to the main road about a hundred and fifty yards higher up than Jones's avenue. There was a bus-stop opposite. A bus to the city-centre had just pulled away from it. I hadn't a hope of catching it.

There aren't many buses on that route, but I was opposite an avenue which leads down to another main bus-route about half-a-mile away. Crossing the road I would be in full view of anyone who might come out of Jones's avenue. On the other hand anyone who noticed me where I was, lurking in the shadow of the hedge, would immediately become suspicious. I walked boldly across the road. I couldn't make up my mind what to do. I was half-tempted to nip into one of the gardens and lie low for a while. But if I were caught in somebody's garden it would look very suspicious. I'd be brought along for Miss Jones to identify and even if nothing could be proved Jones would give me the sack first thing in the morning. He'd have every right to. After all I'm cashier in the firm. No one could be expected to entrust money to a person caught lurking in somebody else's garden at night.

I stood at the bus-stop for about half-a-minute. I felt horribly obvious. There didn't seem to be another soul about. Anyone looking for a young man of medium height and slim build would immediately spot me. Once Jones saw me he'd want to know what I was doing at this end of town. It would be no good saying I had been visiting friends. The police would want to know *what* friends. . . . And if I said I'd just been out for a walk that would sound pretty thin. There are plenty of good walks about home.

I lost my nerve and began to walk down the avenue that leads to the other bus-route. I heard a car behind me. A big car! A police car? I expected it to pull up beside me and policemen to jump out and start questioning me. I still had no idea what to say. The car went on. It wasn't a police car. It wasn't even particularly big. Then it came to me—what to say, I mean. I had been seeing a girl. No I was not prepared to say who she was. I'd get away with *that* all right. Everyone would believe me straight away—and Jones would think I was far more of a lad than he'd ever imagined.

I walked on, but no one stopped me. I caught a bus on the other road and reached home safely without further adventure.

Jones has been rather amusing about 'The Marauder', as he calls him. That means me of course. But Jones doesn't know. He has two quite different stories, which taken together, don't make sense. Whoever is listening to him is expected to believe both stories. One is that a sexual maniac made an attack on his daughter. Some chap

with wild eyes and a beard. The other is that somebody was trying
to get into his garage to steal his car. He likes both stories. So do I.
The police haven't a chance. They are looking for a wild-eyed man
with a beard, whereas I am clean-shaven with mild, rather weak
eyes. I don't mean that I have to wear spectacles. Just if people
look hard at me my eyes water and I feel uncomfortable. I'm the
sort of person you'd think wouldn't say 'Boo' to a goose, but you'd
be wrong. I nearly always say 'Boo' to geese when I meet them,
provided there's no one else there of course.

It appears that for the last few months some man has been
frightening women all round Jones's district. Whether the daughter jumped to the conclusion that I was the same man, or whether
the parents put it into her head, I don't know. She never saw my
face, nor I hers. But the police need evidence. If it's not there it has
to be manufactured.

One thing is obvious. I shall have to put off my attack on Jones's
tyres until the autumn. Jones is now alert. He and his neighbours
are on the look-out for suspicious characters. I rather hope they
catch the chap with the beard, or else that he gives up his little
games. Meantime the whole district is unsafe for any man who
can't explain exactly what he is doing. But I'd have had to put it off
till the autumn anyhow. I need darkness and I need to go and come
in the bus. The buses stop shortly after eleven. About the end of
October would seem to be the right time.

The sex-chap *has* been caught. Just one week after my affair. I
suppose this is a good thing for me. All the same I feel sorry for
the poor blighter. What harm did he actually do anyone? Frightful scandal, of course, all hushed up. This means the whole town
knows, but the police aren't brought in. Some respected local
resident, retired bank manager or something. I'm not important
enough for Jones to tell me the story directly, but he told the Book-
keeper. It appears the old boy hadn't a beard any more than I have.
Just wore a muffler, either to keep out the cold, or as a disguise.
He's to get psychiatric treatment.

Jones is disappointed. He doesn't think it's the same man. The
man who attacked his daughter had a black beard and wild eyes.
He was a big, powerful chap and quite young. As soon as Jones

appeared he took to his heels and made off like an Olympic champion.

It's funny how he won't give up the idea of the attack on his daughter. I suppose there was more at risk. The car is property and insurable. The sex rights in his daughter are property too, but not insurable, or at any rate not insured. So it is more interesting that his daughter should have been at risk than his car.

There is an old leather travelling bag of Father's which holds nine rats quite comfortably. What I think is called an overnight bag. Nine, I have decided, shall be the team. Two rats for each tyre and Socrates in charge.

Last night I had what I call a training session. I went up to the shed immediately after tea and put the nine rats into the bag. Then straight down the drive and out the gate. As I passed the house I heard Mother tapping at the window with her rings. She shouted, 'Where are you going with Father's bag?' She does this every time I go out with the bag, but I pay no attention—and when I come in again she whines at me. She has got the idea that she is confined to the house. Something the doctor told her. It suits me well enough except that she spends all her time peering out of the windows, trying to find out what I'm up to. She's still as much at sea as ever.

I took a bus into the country, the bag on the floor between my feet. There wasn't the slightest movement from it. None of the other passengers could have guessed it held anything living. Yet when I lift it I can tell from the feel that there are rats inside. It feels different from a bag filled with pyjamas and a spare shirt and shaving things. I smiled to myself going along in the bus. If the other passengers knew what was in my bag! If I opened it, what a scene! I was tempted to open it. I had the greatest difficulty in resisting the temptation.

I got off at a spot which you might describe as truly rural. I walked up a pleasant country road. I looked for a nice, dry bank, where I could sit down and let the rats out for a little run. Almost anywhere would have done. All I needed was that there should be no one about. I walked on for a little, partly because it was a pleasant evening, looking for the perfect spot.

I came round a corner and found a chap and a girl in a parked car. I felt annoyed. Either I had to go back a bit or go further than I had intended. I reflected on the situation. Some animals have a mating season, some like men and rats, keep at it all the year round. I walked past pretending not to peer in. I had lascivious thoughts. Then I thought, 'Ha-ha. I'll make them pay for their fun and games.'

Whether they even noticed me I don't know. At any rate I didn't have the slightest effect on their goings-on. I realised suddenly that here was a perfect chance for a full-dress rehearsal. About twenty yards further up the road behind the car was a field-gate. I opened it and went in. Then I came back behind the hedge till I was just beside the car, with only the ditch between us. I opened the bag and let the rats out. For a few minutes I stroked them all, particularly Socrates, and let them run over me. Then I whispered, 'Tyres. Tear 'em up,' and lifted up Socrates so that he could see the car through the hedge.

Socrates led the others through a little gap in the bottom of the hedge. The ditch was dry. They crossed in single file and the attack began, two each to three of the tyres, Socrates helping with the fourth. I watched to see how they would get on. They took it turn about, one gnawing and clawing furiously for fifteen seconds or so, then the other taking over, and so on.

They didn't go for the thick part of the tyres. They did what I had taught them to do on the old covers at home. They went for the tyre-walls, the thinnest part just above the bulge. And they worked on a very small area, so that they could make a deep cut surprisingly quickly.

Everything was going well, the chap and the girl quite regardless of what was happening. Suddenly there was a great hiss. Socrates and his lot were through first. Not surprising seeing they'd an extra mouth on the job. 'What's that?' said the chap.

'Sounds like a tyre,' said the girl.

'Sisss, sisss, sisss,' said the tyre.

You could almost hear them listening to it. It's funny what it takes to upset people. I nearly split myself trying not to laugh.

The rats on the off-side back got through. Another hiss started up. A different note from the first one, fresh and vigorous. By this time the first one had begun to have a sort of dying fall. At any rate it was quite easy to distinguish that there were now two hisses instead of one.

'I say, what *is* this?' said the chap. 'Is someone letting our tyres down?'

He opened the door and peered out. At the same time the girl opened the window at her side and peered out too. 'It's rats,' the chap exclaimed. 'They're eating the tyres.' I liked the mixture of wonder and fear in his voice—awe.

'Oh, Bert, it's the same this side. They'll be eating us next.'

Bert believed her instantly. He jumped out of the car and raced down the road.

The girl burst into tears. 'Oh Bert,' she called after him. 'You wouldn't leave me to be eaten alive by rats.'

But he had. When he got to what he thought a safe distance— and he was taking no risks—he looked round and found that the rats were not actually at his heels. In fact they were still at the car. He shouted back, 'Shut the door so they don't get in on you. I'll get help.'

I made a special noise, a sort of 'Cluck-cluck-cluck,' which you wouldn't know was human. It means 'Come to me at once.' There was still one tyre holding out, but this time one didn't matter. The rehearsal had gone perfectly. I don't mean to do Jones's tyres when anyone's there. He'll go for his car in the morning and find out then what's happened to it.

The rats came back through the hedge. The girl was now standing on the seat. I was terrified she'd catch sight of me. I lay very still. I don't think she saw me. But she still saw the rats. 'Bert,' she called, 'they're going away.' She hopped out of the car and rushed after him.

Bert, all danger past, had at least the grace to wait for her. She flung herself into his arms and laid her head on his manly shoulder. 'Oh Bert. I got such a fright.'

I bet she did.

Extraordinary. You'd think she'd have had enough of Bert. Not a bit of it. They went off with their arms round each other, all lovey-dovey, to look for help. All the same she'll take it out of him once they're married.

I was afraid they'd come back to investigate and find me crouching behind the hedge. But no. Definitely not the stuff that heroes are made of.

I put the rats back in the bag and started towards the main road to catch the bus home. After a bit I met Bert and the girl and a chap with a pitchfork. 'Did you see any rats?' the pitchfork-chap asked, giving a great yokel-grin.

'Rats!' I repeated, all innocence. 'No. I don't think so.'

'They attacked our car,' said the girl. 'Hundreds of them. They'd have eaten us if they could.'

'Really?' I sounded quite incredulous.

'That's right,' Bert said. 'They ate the tyres off the car. It'd have been us next if they could have got us.'

They actually believed there were hundreds of rats. It's like Jones and his marauder.

I took the bus home to Mother. As usual I had to listen to a lot of questions, but I told her nothing. She is getting very frail. I don't think she'll live much longer.

It is strange how I have come to love Socrates. I sit for hours just playing with him and stroking his fur. Sometimes it seems to me that he is more intelligent than a human being. At any rate he is more congenial to me. Of course he's no ordinary rat. I think that perhaps he belongs to a new species. The only difference I can be sure of is the tail. Ordinary rats have fleshy, scaly tails, which are rather horrid. Socrates, and one or two of the other young ones, have long, furry tails. They begin thin and pink, like a mouse's tail, and get furry later. I think Socrates is proud of his. When he is moving about it is usually straight out behind him and slightly raised so that it doesn't trail on the ground. At other times he carries it at an angle, rather like a cat, but Socrates' tail is never quite straight up. He keeps it very clean, but then he is a very clean animal.

Yesterday was Sunday and I got up early so as to have plenty of time with him before church. We had been out late the night before and he didn't hear me when I went into the shed. For quite a time I just stood there watching him sleeping, his tail curled round him. It seemed cruel to wake him. I reasoned with myself a little before I did so. Sleep is temporary death. For Socrates life is good.

He likes it when I play with him. Therefore I should wake him up, bring him from death to life. And of course this morning I too had been glad to wake, because it was Sunday and I should have a long time with Socrates. Most mornings I would rather be asleep than awake. I hate getting up and going into business. Does that mean I prefer death to life?

Anyhow I decided to wake Socrates. I whistled. Socrates opened his eyes. His tail uncurled slowly. He stood up and stretched. Then he saw me. I knew he saw me by the expression on his face. It was a rather comic expression, a mixture of sleepiness and reproach, and a sort of shamefacedness at not being up and about—as if he were saying, 'Well you know the way it is. We all sleep in occasionally.'

However he was not going to neglect his toilet on my account. He sat down and began to wash his face. It was no skimped wash either. He went from his face to behind his ears, to his back, to his sides, to his tummy, licking his hands all the time to keep them wet. Next he licked his hind feet and scratched himself with them. So he went on till he got right down to the end of his tail, licking and biting that. Not till every minute portion of him was licked or scratched or bitten did he consent to come over to me and let me talk to him and stroke him.

I have never felt towards any human being as I feel towards Socrates. I had the same feeling towards a dog we had when I was a child. The dog was poisoned eventually. Something I never forgot, or forgave. That dog was my best friend. I used to let him lick my face for five or ten minutes at a time. It was delightful. I can still remember the warm, rough-smooth feeling of his tongue, the way I had to dry my face with my handkerchief when it was over.

When I was even smaller I loved Mother with a love that was very intense. I suppose I still love her, but I am not conscious of it. She irritates me extremely. For years, it seems, she has done nothing but nag at me. Any feelings of tenderness and love I have are therefore directed towards Socrates. There is no one else.

I have made a house for Socrates. A sort of doll's house, I suppose you'd call it. Anyhow it's inside the tool-shed, and it's got electric light. It's wonderful what you can do if you try. I've no experience of carpentry or working with electricity, but there it is. It's not really separate like a doll's house. You can't lift it up and take it away. It's built into a corner of the tool-shed, on the bench. It's even got heating. I bored holes in the bench with a brace and bit and fitted a sort of box below. Inside the box I put a tin with an electric light bulb in it. When you switch on, the bulb heats the tin and warm air flows up through the holes in the bench into the house. I had some difficulty getting switches which would turn on and off easily enough to be worked by a rat. However by dint of fiddling with them a bit I have managed to fit switches that Socrates can work. I have had to be very careful. I don't want any short circuits which might start a fire. Another difficulty was to make Socrates understand about the heater. He learned to work the light switches very quickly, because these gave instant results. But it's quite a time before the heater begins to take effect. I had to demonstrate it time after time. He tumbled to it in the end, but what a job! The whole electricity supply comes from a plug in the garage. I'm sure the electricity people wouldn't approve of it, but they shan't ever see it. There's nothing wrong with it really. The part outside is lead-covered cable and I've put it underground.

There's Mother calling, I wonder what she wants now. She thinks I should spend all my spare time with her, running little messages, listening to her reminiscences.

You'd think that by this time I should be able to write a book about rats, but in fact I know very little about them. Of course I know Socrates very well, and from time to time, I still see his mother. Apart from that there are about twenty other rats which I can recognise as individuals. All of these are, I think, males. I can't be sure, because I still can't see any difference between males and females. It's just that none of them has ever had any appearance of carrying young.

All these rats I have tried to train. With about a dozen I have had some success. The others are failures who keep coming to the shed in the hope of getting a share of the scraps I bring. I would like to get rid of the failures, but I don't like actually to chase them. The rats obviously trust me and I don't want to destroy that trust, though eventually I shall have to make some sort of selection.

The successful rats have all one physical characteristic in common, furry tails. I don't know if this means that there are normally two different types of rat, one with furry tails and one with scaly tails, or whether the furry tails are just a peculiarity of the Socrates family. Socrates' mother has the ordinary scaly tail and so I think have his brothers and sisters. The trouble is I don't know which *are* his brothers and sisters. I'm inclined to think all the scaly-tailed rats who hang round are brothers and sisters, but I'm not sure. This leads me to wonder if all the furry-tailed rats are Socrates' children. It is certainly Socrates who brings them along. At least I think it is. I don't see them arrive. From time to time I come in and find a new young rat with Socrates. The new one stays close to Socrates for a day or two. Then it joins the others. Perhaps he just brings along the brightest rat out of each litter. Horrifying thought! This would mean that Socrates would have had a dozen families in the comparatively short time I have known him.

There is one other thing about the furry-tailed rats which I think is different. I think they have slightly larger heads and perhaps larger eyes, but I'm not sure. I don't know how you'd set about measuring the size of their heads—and eyes would be impossible to measure.

The difficulty about getting to know anything about rats is that so much of their life goes on underground. I don't know if my rats—the rats I know—are part of a large colony or just a family group. If there's a colony I don't know what they live on. So far as food's concerned I think most rats must have a pretty poor time. This means that rats have a poor time in general. I mean when you get down to it food is the main thing in life. You won't get far without it.

Tonight when I went to the shed there was a big scaly-tailed rat there. I knew at once that the other rats were hostile to it. I would have liked to chase it away, but I didn't. Partly I was afraid. It's a big rat. I thought if I tried to chase it it might attack me. If it did I don't know what the other rats would do. I imagine they would take my side, but I'm not sure. Perhaps their loyalty to their species would be stronger than their loyalty to me. If all the rats in the shed, twenty or so, went for me at once I don't think I'd have much chance. I saw what they did to the tyres. I am certainly not as tough as the cover of a motor tyre.

So I took no action. I carried on as if the strange rat was not there. I put out the food for the furry-tailed rats. This is always a bit of a problem in any case. The regular scaly-tailed rats always get some of it, though I try to ensure that their share is as little as possible. If only the rats would eat the food where I give it to them this would not be difficult. But they won't. They insist on taking it away and eating it close to the wall, preferably in a corner. An artificial corner does as well as a real one. I mean if they can get behind a box or something they are perfectly happy. I can understand this feeling. When I go into a restaurant I don't like a table in the middle of the floor. I like to be against a wall or in a corner or behind a pillar. In a rat restaurant there would be no tables in the middle of the floor.

When a new young rat comes along with Socrates I make a point of giving him something directly out of my hand. He then endeavours to take it away to some secluded spot to eat it. As often as not he is set upon by the older scaly-tailed rats who roll him over on his back and take it from him. So far as I can see the rat which is attacked is not hurt in any way, but the method of attack is always the same and the young rat submits to it without any apparent attempt to fight back. As the young rat grows up, which doesn't take long, these attacks gradually cease. It surprises me a little that Socrates never interferes. At first I expected him to come to the help of his young hopefuls, but he never paid the slightest attention.

This new rat however is an adult and under nobody's protection. It is obviously completely on its own. I wondered what would happen. I waited till Socrates and some of his family were well away from the newcomer. Then I put down some bits of bread and cabbage in front of them. Immediately the big rat came pushing forward. He didn't exactly dash forward. He moved quickly and at the same time with a sort of deliberation and force as if nothing would put him off his course. Yet he didn't get the food. The other rats snapped at him, and crowded in front of him. By the time he got to where the food had been it was all gone. It had all gone to the furry-tailed rats. I wondered then if the scaly-tailed rats accepted the fact that the furry-tailed ones get priority. Thinking back I am inclined to think they do, in spite of robbing the young ones. What it amounts to is that my favour for the furry-tailed is taken by the others as a right the furry-tailed ones have acquired. The furry-tails form an aristocracy, perhaps a priestly caste. The scaly-tails instead of siding with the intruder, who is scaly-tailed like themselves, support the system which is in power.

After a time all the furry-tails had been fed. The scaly-tails had all got a little, except the newcomer. In spite of his size he had been kept off. What's more he seemed to accept this in a sad sort of way. He made no attempt to fight for food. Yet obviously he was very hungry. At last I took pity on him and deliberately gave him the last bit of cabbage stalk. I kept the others away while he ate it.

After this I started 'Lessons' as usual. 'Lessons' are only for the furry-tails. The others take no part and don't attempt to interfere. 'Lessons' are simply teaching the rats to understand what I say. Teaching them the names of things is by now pretty easy, but to order them about I need to teach them a lot more than that.

The big rat got in the way. When I said, 'Go into the watering-can,' he went too, without in the least understanding—he just followed the others. And when I said, 'Now come back to the bench,' he was in the way. They had to heave him out of the mouth of the watering-can. Then he followed them to the bench. In all this the other scaly-tailed rats took no part. They just watched.

I didn't do much more. In fact I'm not sure what I want to teach them. I've got a vague sort of idea that I ought to be able to get some advantage from my trained rats. I could train more and more until I had quite an army. Surely I could do something with an army of rats. Of course I could exhibit them. People would probably pay to see performing rats, but I wouldn't like that. I mean going on the stage and that sort of thing. I don't like anything public. Surely I could get rats to do things for me, things nobody else could do. But what? I can't think of a single thing, except the tyres on Jones's car, and it won't be dark enough for that for another fortnight.

Last night I pinched a huge leek from Major Robinson's garden down the road. It's wonderful how easy it is to pinch the odd thing from people's gardens. Who's going to miss one leek? Of course I did it after dark and then I had to boil it without Mother seeing. I waited till she'd gone to bed.

Tonight I'd meant to give the rats a lesson in co-operation, but the big rat spoiled it. He's really becoming a nuisance. I went out immediately after tea and got the leek from where I'd hidden it, above the door of the coal-house in the yard. The moon was shining and it was quite bright. I took the leek up the garden and put it down between the shed and the greenhouse, right out in the open. I knew the rats wouldn't want to eat it in the open. They'd want to drag it away into shelter of some kind.

When I felt that the leek was in the absolute centre of the space, equi-distant from the shed, the greenhouse, the frames and the hedge, I went back to the shed for Socrates. I carried him out and put him down beside the leek. All the other rats came with me, the furry-tailed ones close to my feet, the regular scaly-tailed ones a little behind, and the big intruder ranging up and down, not accepted by either group.

My object was to persuade the furry-tails to co-operate and drag the leek right round the shed and in the door. Inside the shed was the only place where they could be really safe from all marauders. But it was the longest haul.

At first, as I had expected, the furry-tails gathered round the leek and all began to pull in different directions. 'Stop!' I said sharply. 'Food to shed.'

They were puzzled. All the furry-tails understood the words I had used. But they didn't connect them. I don't know if the scaly-tails understood anything or not. They were just waiting in the background to see if there would be any of the leek over when the furry-tails had finished with it. After a moment two of the furry-tails set off for the shed without the leek. The others watched me. If I had done nothing more they might all have gone back to the shed, or they might have attacked the leek again and torn it to pieces. 'No,' I called. I picked up one end of the leek and began to drag it slowly along the ground. 'Take—food—to—shed.' I emphasised each word.

Socrates of course tumbled to it first. He jumped forward,

caught the leek and walking backwards began to tug it along in the direction of the door of the shed. I immediately let go. 'Good,' I told Socrates.

'Good' is a word they all understand. Several of the furry-tails went at once to Socrates' help. The others joined in. There wasn't room for all of them actually on the leek, but they gathered round and the leek moved slowly and steadily towards the tool-shed door. The scaly-tails followed at a respectful distance. It was like a funeral, with the leek as the coffin, the furry-tails as the bearers and the scaly-tails as the general body of mourners.

Then the decorum of the proceedings was suddenly upset. The big scaly-tailed intruder darted in, seized the trailing end of the leek and began to tug it in the opposite direction. For a moment the furry-tails were bewildered. I was annoyed, but amused at the same time. The delay was only for a moment. The furry-tails gathered round the intruder and pushed him off, snapping at him, but not so far as I could see actually biting him. The intruder didn't snap back. He made one or two more attempts to dart in at the leek, but they were not successful.

Then I noticed a funny noise. At first I didn't know what it was, a sort of high speed rattling, not very loud, but very sharp. It came in bursts, like a sort of miniature machine-gun, only the bursts lasted longer and the sound was thinner. It had an instant effect on the rats. They all froze—and then I realised it was Socrates. His teeth were chattering. I couldn't think what had happened to him. I wondered had he suddenly gone mad or hysterical. At the same time I was slightly frightened, or at least uneasy. If the other rats hadn't been there I might have stroked him or picked him up. Probably it's just as well I didn't. I think it was something in the attitude of the other rats which prevented me. The chattering went on in bursts for two or three minutes. All that time none of the other rats moved.

When it stopped they all moved very quickly—all except Socrates and the big brown rat. You couldn't say the others made a ring. There wasn't a ring, but all the rats except Socrates and the big brown rat, had moved out of the way. It was a sort of sudden shuffle and there they were with the deck cleared for action, so to speak. Socrates and the big rat about two and a half feet apart, with the leek, deserted, between *them* and the other rats.

Socrates had another spell of teeth chattering.

The big rat nibbled at the ground as if he had found a grain of food there or something, but I don't think he had. I think he was just nervous.

Socrates' teeth stopped chattering. He took a step or two towards the big rat. His hair was standing on end. He shitted and pissed. The other rat shitted too, but I didn't notice whether he pissed or not. I thought Socrates was going to go for the other rat straight away, but he didn't. He arched his back and began to circle round the other one with little short steps as if he were dancing on his toes. He didn't seem to be looking at the other rat, though of course rats look sideways. Anyhow he kept his side towards the big one. He went right round him twice and all the time the big rat never moved, except for his little nibbling at something on the ground.

Next Socrates leaped into the air. He came down on the big rat's back. His jaws snapped. He seemed to bite the big rat's ear. There was a moment of flurry. The big rat shook his head and seemed to try to get away. He didn't fight back. He half rolled over and in a moment they were apart again, both quite still, waiting. I suppose they stayed like that for a minute, maybe a little longer. Then very slowly the big rat moved away, six inches, a foot, two feet, three feet, four feet. There he stopped. 'Shoo,' I said, but he went no further. He was already separated from the other rats, an outcast, a leper.

For a long time nothing happened. Presently one of the furry-tails began to nibble at the leek. 'No!' I called. 'Stop! Leek to shed.' Immediately I corrected myself, 'Food to shed.' I repeated it several times. 'Food to shed. Food to shed.'

Socrates was the first to recover his wits. He picked up his end of the leek again and began to drag it towards the shed as if nothing had happened. Good old Socrates. Victorious in battle against a far bigger opponent. Like David and Goliath. 'Lucky you didn't get killed,' I said to Goliath. 'Yeller, aren't you!' I felt quite proud of Socrates.

The other furry-tails began to help again, pulling the leek along. The scaly-tails followed, but did nothing. Once more it was like a funeral, a funeral with one mourner who couldn't quite keep up. The big rat trailed dismally along about two feet behind the last of the other scaly-tails.

They got the leek round the corner and in through the door of the shed. As soon as the last of our own rats was in I shut the door. The big rat was left outside. That'll teach him to come poking his nose in where he's not wanted.

The reason I saw all this so clearly was because there was a full moon. It was almost as bright as day.

Going up to the shed this evening it was dark and there was a slight drizzle. I couldn't see a thing. I stumbled over something that felt soft and rather horrid. I had a torch with me. I put it on and shone it on the ground. There was a big, dead rat lying right in the middle of the path. I felt sure at once that it was the big rat Socrates had fought the other night. I turned it over gingerly to try to see what had happened to it, but there was no mark on it except a little dried blood on the ear. Perhaps it was poisoned. I hope not. If there is poison about my furry-tails might get it. I wouldn't mind about the scaly-tails. If we could get rid of all of *them* I should be delighted.

Jones gets smugger every day. He's so *pleased* with himself. It just oozes out of him. I gather the firm has had a good year and of course he thinks he's done it all himself. So he has in a way, by sweating it out of the rest of us and keeping us at starvation wages. All the same he'll get a queer shock when he finds his tyres torn to pieces. It will make him feel unsafe. The tyres one night, maybe Jones himself some other night. I don't mean that's what'll happen. I mean that's what he'll think. If he doesn't, I'll put it into his head.

The time approaches.

Mother was late with tea. Tonight of all nights! But it was the second time recently. It always used to be on the table prompt at half-past six. It's no good complaining. She'd just tell me she wasn't brought up to this sort of thing, meaning that when she was young, fifty years ago, they kept a cook, a parlourmaid, housemaids, kitchenmaid, bootboy and all the rest of it. Back to that I suppose would be her idea of heaven. Send up someone from hell to do a bit of scrubbing. But apparently in heaven it's the angels who do the chores, while the few humans who make it just hang about it taking it easy, like the Victorian upper classes.

After tea of course I had to help with the washing up. I always do. Mother washes and I dry. We've always done it that way, but it means I have to wait for her. And was she slow? I don't know whether she does it deliberately to keep me talking or if it's just another sign that she's getting old.

At last we were finished. I dashed into the hall and grabbed my hat and waterproof. Mother came doddering after me. 'Are you going out, dear? It's not a very nice evening.'

Of course I was going out. What did she think I wanted my coat and hat for. But I just said, 'Yes,' quite politely.

'Well don't be too late, will you? I never get to sleep till I know you're in.'

'No.'

As she says she never gets any sleep anyway I don't know what difference my being in or out can make.

I rushed up to the shed. I'd some bits of liver in my pocket as a special treat for Socrates and the other furry-tails. They like liver. Of course they're not dependent on *me* for food. At least I hope not. I don't know how much a rat eats. But I count that I just provide a few extras, usually scraps from the house. The liver was an exception. I'd bought it with my own money (I mean not the housekeeping) in a cooked meat shop in town. I never really mean to feed the scaly-tails at all. Only it can't be helped. They're there. Tonight I was in a generous mood. I gave them a few bits of bread to keep them quiet.

I didn't know what to do about the liver. My idea was that the team should eat it before we set off and travel with full stomachs. That way they'd feel warm and comfortable, and be less likely to make a noise in the bag. Not that they often do. They're almost always very good. Just I wanted to take all precautions. This was where the time question came in. If I gave them the liver first, we'd be late starting and maybe not get the job done soon enough to catch the last bus home. Besides if they'd full stomachs they might get sleepy and not want to attack the tyres.

So I compromised and let them eat half, which they did fairly quickly. Then I popped them into the bag and showed them the rest as a promise of more good things to come.

I set off with the bag in my hand. I went down to the bus-stop and caught a bus to the City Centre. No trouble in that bus. No trouble in the bus out to where Jones lives.

9.15. I got off the bus at the stop nearest the end of Jones's avenue—about twenty-five yards away. I thought the conductor gave me a funny look, but I'm not sure. Maybe he was wondering what was in my bag.

I walked up the avenue feeling excited, but confident. Solid red-brick houses on either side, probably built about nineteen-ten. Most of the people were in their front rooms. Some had the curtains across, heavy curtains with the light just showing through. In other houses you could see in. Perhaps they like to be seen, show how well off they are, so other people can envy them. Standard lamps, polished tables, chintz-covered furniture, subdued light, cosy glow from the fire. It was drizzling slightly, more like a mist really. I felt it cold against my cheeks and my eyelashes were wet.

I wondered if Jones would have his curtains across or not. It would be funny to see Jones at his own fireside in the bosom of his family. He'd never guess who was looking in at him. I wondered what he did in the evenings. Read? Talk? Probably both. He reads every line in the evening paper, the things about the child born with ducks' feet in Arizona and the calf with two heads in Brazil. I thought I'd like to see Jones's daughter, the one who caught me at the garage door, not that she actually caught me. It would be funny if she were pretty. I mean with Jones as her father.

But Jones cheated me. The curtains were across and I couldn't see a thing. Worse still. The lights were on in the garage and the door was closed. Jones must be in there, working. Footering about more likely. If he stayed there long I'd just have to turn round and go home again.

At first I didn't know how to shift him. Then I thought of a ruse. I remembered a telephone box on the main road, near the bus-stop. I was now about fifty yards past Jones's house. I'd keep on walking in case of someone coming out and seeing a suspicious figure, palely loitering. But in fact the avenue was quite deserted.

Extraordinary how quiet the suburbs can be at times. You could cut someone's throat in the middle of the road and no one would notice. If he yelled they'd just think it was cats.

I walked down the avenue again very quickly. Time was getting on. I'd have liked to run. But you couldn't tell. Someone peering from an upstairs window, might see me under a street lamp. A man with a bag, running. A suspicious character. Phone the police! As I reached the main road a bus went by quite empty. Even the conductor was sitting down reading the paper. The phone-box was empty too. Every house has its own phone. If you economised by doing without a phone, you'd economise by living somewhere else.

I had begun to feel the weight of the bag. I was quite glad to put it down for a bit inside the phone-box. 'All right children,' I said soothingly. 'You'll get out soon now.' I decided to leave the bag open while I telephoned, in case the rats were too hot and needed air. There they all were good as gold. They hardly even moved when the light shone in on them, but I saw Socrates looking up at me, just waiting to be told what to do. Bless his little heart.

I know Jones's number in my head. I've had to get it for him sometimes in the office, when the operator is out for her lunch or off sick or something. Of course Jones is too important now ever to get a number for himself. I dialled, heard it begin to ring and before anyone could answer put in my four pennies. The moment the receiver was lifted I pressed Button A. I held my nose so that when I spoke I'd have an American accent.

A woman answered, 'Hello.' Rather snooty. His good lady, as he calls her.

'Hallo there,' I said.

I waited a moment and Mrs. Jones said, 'Hello,' again. Not so snooty this time. My nasal voice had made her interested.

I went on, 'Hallo there. That you Liverpool? New York here.' I stopped again. Someone told me once that all the New York calls came through Liverpool. I don't know why.

Mrs. Jones was really interested by this time. 'Hello, hello! Hello?'

I didn't want her to hang up yet. 'Just a minute, Philadelphia. I'm talking to Liverpool here, Liverpool, England. Can you hear me, Liverpool?'

'I can hear you very well,' Mrs Jones replied, 'but I'm afraid it's not Liverpool.'

'Sorry ma'am. I'm trying to get Liverpool to get me a Mr. Jones, but they've gotten hung up or sumf'n.' Not good enough to convince an American perhaps, but Mrs. Jones and I have probably the same idea of an American accent. Why anyhow should she have been suspicious?

She wasn't. She's proud and British. It's not every day she gets a call from New York. 'This is the Jones residence.'

I hung up. I knew she'd have Jones in in two ticks. A call from New York coming through. He'd hang about waiting for it. He'd be tickled to death. He once did have a real call from New York and he didn't stop blowing about it for ages.

I closed the bag, picked it up, and hurried back. All the houses just the same. Not a soul about. Nothing changed. Yes there was, though. Jones's garage doors were open, the light streaming out. I looked at my watch. A quarter to ten. No time to waste. But Jones might still be there on the other side of the car, bending over it, or crouched down doing something to one of the wheels.

I'd have to chance it. I opened the gate. This time it squeaked like evermore. What if Jones heard and came popping out of the garage to see who was there? There was so much light he'd be bound to recognise me. Even if he didn't and I turned and bolted, I didn't stand a chance carrying that bag. He'd think it was *The Marauder* again and come tearing after me, yelling his head off to attract the neighbours. I'd have to face it out, think up some sort of excuse. 'Oh hello, Mr. Jones. Very mild isn't it for the time of year. I was looking for some people called McEllhenny, friends of ours. This bag belongs to them and Mother insisted on me coming over to return it.' A bit awkward if there were McEllhennys next door. But it wasn't likely. There aren't an awful lot of McEllhennys about. Anyhow they could have turned out to be the wrong McEllhennys. I'd have said I was looking for the Theophilus McEllhennys. I'm sure *they*'d take a bit of finding.

But Jones didn't appear. I got off the crunchy gravel and approached the garage door stealthily. I put down the bag. I got right down flat on the ground and peered into the garage. No feet, no legs showing on the far side of the car. All clear in fact. He *must* have gone to the phone. I picked up the bag and walked boldly in. I opened the bag and took out the rats. 'Tear it up! Tear it up!' Two rats to each tyre. 'Tear it up! Tear it up.' I kept Socrates with me. Whatever happened I didn't want *him* hurt.

I looked at my watch again. Ten to ten. I'd been quicker than I thought. All action of course.

I went out again and hid behind a bush in the garden where I could see the front door, and at the same time get clear away to the gate if I had to run for it. I watched and waited, stroking Socrates and whispering to him to pass the time. 'He's a bad cruel man, Socrates. He deserves everything that happens to him. He wouldn't let us have enough to eat if he had his way. He only pays starvation wages. And look at the way he lives himself. Doesn't skimp when it comes to looking after Mr. Jones as you can see for yourself.'

Five to ten. I thought it would have been more. Was Jones still hanging about the phone? Perhaps he was reading the paper to put in the time. But how long would he wait before he decided to go back to the garage and finish whatever he was doing, or else close up for the night? 'Dear me,' he'd say to Mrs. Jones any minute now. 'That call's a long time. I've left the garage open, and the light on! I think I'll just pop out and lock up. Give me a shout if they come through again.' 'Yes certainly, dear,' Mrs. Jones would say and out he'd come all fuss.

Ten o'clock. Surely the rats should be nearly finished by now. Of course rubber's tough and there are only two of them to each tyre. I never timed them before. I suppose I should have. I'd have been better to do only one tyre. It would have been quite enough to impress Jones. I could have let them go at it in shifts. All the same four tyres ruined will impress him even more.

Five past ten. I could bear it no longer. I went in to see how they were getting on. Air hissing. They'd done it. I should have realised they'd go on gnawing till I told them to stop, puncture or no puncture. I checked quickly. One tyre flat. One almost flat. One just through and doing most of the hissing. One not quite through. I pulled out my pocket-knife and administered the coup de grace to that one myself. We'd been too long already.

And then I heard a door close. I'd never heard it open. Jones's step on the gravel. In another second he'd be in on top of me. And no amount of McEllhennys could explain this away. I noticed a small door at the back of the garage. Perhaps we were saved. 'Stop!' I whispered desperately to the rats. 'Here!' They came. But what slow movers they are. Even at full speed rats are slow. I almost threw them into the bag. Socrates was there already. All in. I closed the bag, nipped through the small door, and found myself in Jones's back yard. Dark. I felt about, tripped over the bin, discovered another door, opened it—and emerged into the garden. I tiptoed round the back of the garage. What *was* Jones doing? Ah! The open gate had caught his eye, and annoyed him no doubt, careful householder that he is. He had closed it and was now approaching the front door of the garage. Would he close that also and go away without noticing his ripped tyres? I froze. He closed one half. The light was still on. He had to step inside to switch it off.

'What the hell!'

He'd noticed. What next?

For a long time he did nothing. His footsteps had stopped. He must have been just staring into the garage wondering what had happened to his car. 'It looks odd, doesn't it, *Mister* Jones? Sort of sunk down.' Ah! A step. He'd gone in a little. Not very far. Some maniac had slashed his tyres. The maniac might still be lurking near, ready to jump out and rip up Jones as well as his tyres. Jones was frightened. So was I. If I made the slightest movement Jones would hear me and shout for help. I had cramp in one foot, but I didn't dare more than flex my toes.

Another step. Jones had gathered up a little courage. No he hadn't. He was coming out of the garage, not going further in. I heard the gravel crunch again. He was going back to the house to ring the police. Now should be my chance. As soon as the front door was closed I'd dash out and down to the bus-stop. No one was was going to worry about a respectable young man—well fairly young, and I look younger than my age—standing at the bus-stop with a leather travelling bag in his hand, and once I was on to the bus I'd be safe, whirled away into the city, able to get off wherever I liked.

But the front door didn't shut. Still on tiptoe I got to the side of the garage where I could have a clear run to the gate. The light was streaming out from the hall across the little bit of lawn between the house and the road. 'Emily dear, would you come and look at this, please.' Wish he'd learn to speak like that in the office.

Home is Emily's office. 'Look at what? Don't you know I'm busy?' None of the sweet dignity with which she coos to trans-atlantic telephone operators.

Dare I run for it? I might have got to the gate without being seen, but any moment he might have turned and caught sight of me. Then the chase would have been on. The click of the latch on the gate, the crunch of my foot on the gravel, anything might have attracted his attention. I couldn't run fast with the bag. Better wait a little.

'I want you to look at the tyres on the car. They've been slashed.'

'Slashed! How do you mean slashed?'

'I mean slashed, cut down the sides.'

'Well what good's it going to do, me looking at them? You'd better phone the police.'

Jones pondered over this for a bit. Perhaps he couldn't really believe his tyres had been slashed. Afraid of calling the police and finding that it had all been an illusion. 'Would *you* not phone them?' he said. 'I'll stay here and watch. There may still be someone hang-ing about.'

That was enough for me. Now or never. I'd have to make a bolt for it. Maybe I could get through the hedge at the back and into the garden of a house in the next avenue.

Jones's garden isn't big, but when I got to the back hedge I couldn't hear any longer the conversation between Jones and his sweet Emily. This made me nervous. Though I knew it wasn't pos-sible yet, I felt that the police might be here any second. Perhaps Police H.Q. might already have radioed to one of their roaming patrol cars which might just happen to be in the next avenue. At any moment would come a scream of sirens to alert the whole district.

The hedge at the back wasn't very thick. I burst into it, not caring what harm I did. But there was barbed wire—just one strand, I think. The rest must have rusted away. My trousers caught. I stopped very deliberately, put down the bag in front of me, and unloosed myself. Wouldn't do to have torn pants. Not respectable.

Attract attention immediately. More time gone. I felt increasingly frightened. I almost panicked.

Free at last, in among trees and bushes. A bigger garden than Jones's, classier. I stepped forward cautiously, but caution wasn't much good. I was walking on broken branches and twigs.

'Yap-yap-yap-yap-yap-yap-yap-yap-yap-yap-yap-yap-yap.' The full-stop doesn't mean it did stop. It went on. One of these blasted *little* dogs. A cairn or something, all yap-yap and fury, signifying that it knew jolly well I shouldn't be there and wanted to warn the neighbourhood. I peered out through rhododendrons. I saw a big, square, detached house. There was a broad lawn on one side and the gate on to the road was clearly in view. I couldn't see what was on the other side, probably a yard and garage with more dustbins to trip over. The dog was on the back lawn, about six feet away. He was afraid to come into the shrubbery because of the awful monster lurking there. I tried to think what to do. I could either dash straight across the lawn to the gate and get clear, with the chance that someone might open the front door, just as I was passing, and see me. Or I could creep round the other side and perhaps come up against something I didn't expect. In either case I'd have the dog yapping at my heels. Perhaps a good kick would quiet him. On the other hand he might nip me. I didn't want that. I had to make up my mind pretty quickly. If the police came they'd hear the dog yapping and find me straight away. I decided on the quick dash. One, two. . . .

A door opened in the side of the house. Light shone out across the lawn. 'Woofles! Woofles! Don't be nasty to the hedgehogs.'

So I was a hedgehog was I? Better behave like one and stay in the rhododendrons with my bristles up.

'Naughty Woofles. Woofles come to Mother.'

'Yap-yap-yap-yap-yap-yap-yap-yap-yap-yap-yap-yap-yap.'

'Woofles dear, come to Mother. Dear little hedgehogs never harm anybody, only eat up nasty slugs and snails.'

'Yap-yap-yap-yap-yap-yap-yap-yap-yap-yap-yap-yap-yap.'

Woofles' mother gave up. The door closed. I allowed a few seconds to make sure she wouldn't change her mind. Now for it, I thought. I ran across the lawn with the bag in my hand, Woofles yapping and snapping all the way. I reached the gate and got out.

I shut the gate in Woofles' face, but Woofles has a hole in the hedge just beside the gate and was out almost before I'd time to turn round. I was puffed. I couldn't run any more. I began to walk slowly down the avenue towards the main road.

The beastly dog was still with me. 'Woofles, go home!' He paid no attention. He kept jumping at the bag, snapping at *it* rather than me. He must have smelt the rats. If the police came along in one of their big cars they'd be sure to stop to investigate.

'I wonder Sir, would you mind opening your bag and let me see what's inside it.' Not a question, a command. Perhaps he wouldn't even say, 'Sir.' Probably they just put that in books to make everybody think how nice the police are.

'Yap-yap-yap-yap,' and 'Snap-snap-snap-snap.'

Woofles was driving me mad. 'All right,' I shouted suddenly. 'Get in if you want to.' I put the bag down on the pavement and opened it, but Woofles didn't leap bravely in. Not a bit of him. He drew back a little and *looked* in—and barked more furiously than ever. I stood and watched. He got a little closer to the bag. You could hardly see the rats, all huddled in one corner, probably scared out of their wits. But all my better feelings had been lost. I made a dive and grabbed Woofles by the scruff of the neck. I shoved him into the bag with the rats. 'Tear him up!' I said. 'Let the best animal win.' I was quite sure it wouldn't be Woofles. He wouldn't know what to do, shut up in the bag, in the dark, with the rats crawling over him. I walked on a few steps feeling pleased with myself. 'That's fixed you, you little bastard,' I told him. 'No more yappy-yap from you.'

Then I began to feel sorry. Maybe Woofles wasn't such a bad little dog after all. He'd only been doing his duty. To be torn apart by rats would be a horrible death. What would I find when I opened the bag? A half-eaten, dead dog? I put the bag down quickly. Not a sound from inside. I hoped Woofles was still all right. I opened the bag. Woofles jumped out and streaked off home. You never saw a small dog move faster, and not a yap left in him. But what about Socrates and the other rats? I peered in anxiously. All all right. I stroked Socrates for a little. Apparently nobody attacked anybody.

I closed the bag, walked quickly down the avenue and caught a

bus which arrived at exactly the right moment. As I took my seat
I saw a police car turning into Jones's avenue. Neat enough. Safe
enough. Safe home and no more trouble.

Mother is dying. She knows. Indeed I haven't made any attempt
to hide it from her. She wouldn't wish me to. The doctor says she
may last a week or ten days, not more. The sooner the better. If
we had sensible laws the doctor would have chloroformed her last
week as soon as he knew she couldn't recover. In this we are kinder
to our animals than ourselves.

Watching a person die is tedious. It is also interesting. Mother
would like to think that her life had been worth-while. All she
leaves behind her, the only tangible evidence of her struggle with
the world, is me. And she is disappointed in me. I am not the sort
of person I myself would have liked to be. Something has gone
wrong somewhere. But Mother would like to pretend that it hasn't.
She would like to arrive in heaven with a solid record of achievements in her hand, and material achievements at that. 'Look at my
son, down there,' she'd like to be able to say, 'built the business up
to double what it was when his poor father died, and goes to
church twice every Sunday as well. Not that his father didn't do
very well, thanks to having a good wife to look after him and comfort him when he needed it.' Of course I do go to church twice
every Sunday, but once she's dead I won't go at all. I just go now to
save argument.

What Mother does say is this. 'Well dear. When I'm gone you
won't have me to look after you any more.' (Pretty obvious.)
'You'll have to look after yourself.' (Also pretty obvious.) 'You'll
have to look round and find a nice, sensible girl. It's nearly time
you were beginning to think about getting married, but don't be
in too much of a hurry.' (You might say, if I didn't hurry I'd be past
it.) 'Your father always used to say he'd never have got on without
me. If it hadn't been for me he didn't know where he'd have been.
And you've always been a good boy. Never any trouble. You *are* a
good boy, aren't you dear?'

'Yes Mother.'

'She's still wondering what I get up to when I go out at night,
but she's afraid to ask. If there *was* a woman I'm not sure that she'd

mind, so long as she didn't know. She likes a man to be a man, as she told me once, rather surprisingly.

'Well dear, I suppose I've had a good life. A good husband and a good son. I've a great deal to be thankful for.'

I say nothing. She knows she is being a lot of trouble and is rather pathetic about it. Several times I've been late into the office and nearly every day I have to prolong my lunch hour, without always being able to get time to eat anything myself. Not that Mother eats. But she needs things done for her. The district nurse does some of them, but not all. In spite of not eating she keeps vomiting—horrible brown stuff that I have to clear up.

I don't know what to think about Jones. So far as I can hear he hasn't mentioned the destruction of his tyres to anyone. Perhaps the police have told him to say nothing in the hope that the guilty person will give himself away. Don't they know the damage was done by rats? Or is that something so unlikely that it has never occurred to them?

Mother seems to be worrying about what will happen to me after she's dead. I don't know why. She has said several times, 'I hope your uncle will do right by you in the end.' And once she mumbled, 'I'm sure your uncle won't forget his own brother's son.' She means my uncle in Canada, who's supposed to have all the money. He's the only uncle I've got.

I keep watching Jones and sometimes I fancy he is watching me. Does he wonder if it was I who slashed his tyres? I like to think so, but of course I must give him no clue. That's what he's hoping for. It's a sort of duel between us, but he doesn't know that. He thinks I am in his power, that he can crush me at any time.

Jones has been rather nasty about my being late and the time I have been taking for my lunch. 'Can you not get a nurse?' he asks (twice already). 'You can't go on like this or your work will be getting behind.'

'I haven't let my work get behind,' I tell him coldly. 'I've worked late each night till it's done.'

He goes off grumbling.

She died at last. I thought she was never going to. She stuck it three days longer than the doctor thought possible. I must say now that it's over I feel proud of her. She was a tough old bird.

The funeral was this morning. The old-fashioned kind. She didn't want to be cremated. Had to be buried with Father. Gave me special instructions on various occasions over the last fifteen years—every time she had a weak turn or even a bad cold in the head.

There's something about a funeral. It gives you a sense of importance if you're the chief mourner, as I was. Not that I was really mourning a bit. But I liked everyone paying attention to me. I don't suppose I'll have another chance like it. The next funeral in the family will be my own and there won't be many at it. Surprising how many were at Mother's. Mostly from the church, but a few business people as well, friends of Father's. I think old people like going to funerals. The fact that they get back from the graveyard shows that they're still alive themselves.

Jones was there. Very solicitous and quite different from the way he is with me in the office. I think I understand him. He was satisfying his sense of propriety. Father was head of the firm. Mother was Father's widow. By treating Mother's funeral as important he was paying tribute to his own importance and dignity.

That wasn't all. He'd like to buy our house. He grew up in business feeling that Father was someone tremendous. Even if Father wasn't making a great job of things at the end, to Jones he was like the king on his throne. Jones has always wanted to be in the same position. If he could get our house and live in it he'd feel he really had arrived. He looks on it in a funny sort of way as a usurper might look on the royal palace. Well he's not going to get this royal palace if I can help it.

I didn't even let him in after the funeral. He seemed to think we'd all go in and hear a solicitor read Mother's will or something. But I didn't want to let him or anyone else into the house. For one thing I'd nothing to give them. I wasn't going to run about making tea and I couldn't afford drink. So I just let them all go home.

All the same I should have more money now. Mother must have

spent some money on herself. In fact I know she did. All that, even if it isn't very much, is bound to come to me. She hadn't anyone else to leave it to.

I'll bring the rats into the house. I'll put them in the cellar to begin with. Except Socrates. I'll let Socrates go wherever he likes. It will be much handier than having to go up to the shed the whole time. I'll be able to do a lot more about their training.

I went to see the solicitor today. I had to ask Jones to let me out, but he was quite amiable. He still hopes to get the house. I got a terrible shock. Mother had an annuity which died with her. Instead of having more money to keep up the house I'm going to have less. In fact I don't see how I'm going to be able to live. I wonder if Jones knew about the annuity. He may have found something among Father's papers in the office. That would explain why he was so willing to let me out to see the solicitor.

He didn't say anything when I got back, but just as I was going home I ran into him in the passage. He said in a sort of casual way, 'If you're looking for a buyer for that house of your mother's I might be able to help you. I think I know someone who might be interested.'

I think I know the someone too, but he still won't get the house if I can do anything about it.

This evening I started making arrangements for bringing the rats into the house. There are quite a number of problems I have to consider. The rats are not prisoners and I don't intend them to be. If they were prisoners I would have to provide all their food. I couldn't pay for enough food to feed them for more than a day or two and if I started stealing more than the odd vegetable from Major Robinson I would probably get caught. So they have got to be able to get out to find their own food. All that I can offer is comfortable living accommodation with a few tit-bits now and then. For the first week or two I shall feed them fully. I've enough money for that. Then, when they get accustomed to their new quarters, I shall gradually cut down their rations to encourage them to go out and forage for themselves.

The cellar is not completely underground. There is a small grating at the side of the house which opens into it just above ground level. The first thing I had to do was to make an opening in this big enough for a rat to get through. The bars in the grating were each about as thick as a pencil and about the width of a pencil apart. I got a heavy iron bar from the tool-shed and banged at the grating with it till at last I managed to break one of the bars. Then I thrust the heavy bar through and levered it to and fro till I had what I considered a sufficiently large aperture—that is large enough for a full-grown rat, but too small for a cat. The grating is eight feet above the floor of the cellar. The next task will be to build some sort of staircase which the rats can run up and down from the floor of the cellar to the grating and back again.

Well I've got it all fixed up. I found a plank in the tool-shed. I hammered a long nail in at each side leaving the heads of the nails sticking out about a quarter of an inch from the wood. I ran wire round the nails to the unbroken bars of the grating. That supported one end of the plank. The other end is much lower and is supported on the top of an old set of shelves at the opposite side of the cellar. We used to use the shelves for storing apples. I've cut bits out of them so that it will be quite easy for a rat to jump from one shelf to the next, either up or down.

I've made a new house for them out of packing cases. It's beside the shelves so that a rat can go straight into it from any of the bottom three shelves without having to come out on to the cellar floor. I am going to heat it in the same way as I did with Socrates' house in the tool-shed.

I should get it finished tomorrow night and maybe even be able to move them in before bedtime.

The move has been put off for the time being. I got everything done last night as planned, but I'd forgotten to lay in supplies of food. I didn't even know how many rats I had to feed. So I tried to count the furry-tails. I'm not going to bring in the scaly-tails. They can stay outside and look after themselves. I thought there were about twenty furry-tails. When I actually started counting I found the number was more like thirty, perhaps even forty. The trouble is I don't know them all individually, and they never stay still. They're always appearing and disappearing. There are about sixteen I'm really trying to train. The others do get trained a bit too, but by accident.

On thinking it over I don't think I should take even all the furry-tailed ones, just the top twenty. If I want more later I can probably get them all right from the shed. But I shouldn't need to. The ones I take will breed fast enough.

How much will twenty rats eat? A rat weighs about a pound. So twenty rats should eat about as much as one tenth of a human being. In fact I know they eat much more, but how much I have really no idea.

Today during my lunch-hour I went into a shop that calls itself a 'Corn and Feed Store.' I ordered a bag of wheat. 'What's it for?' the man asked.

This seemed to me an impertinence. 'I don't see that that matters,' I answered rather stiffly.

'It matters to the price,' he said. 'If it's for seed or feeding, and if it's for seed what variety, and whether you want it dressed or not, and how.'

'It's for feeding,' I told him.

'You keep fowl?'

I didn't answer this. I feel he must have been trying to make fun of me with his talk about dressing. Apparently no further information was necessary for the fellow weighed up a bag of what I presume is wheat and demanded thirty shillings. It seemed to me a lot, but I wasn't in a position to argue and immediately gave him the money.

'Shall I put it in the car for you?' he enquired.

'No. I want it delivered.' And I was proceeding to give him the address when he interrupted to say, 'We don't deliver. Maybe you'd have the car in tomorrow.'

Of course I had to admit that I have no car. It then turned out that he was able to arrange delivery perfectly well through some delivery service. But for that he wanted another five shillings, if you please. Of course I had to give it to him. I had no choice in the matter. It's dreadful how you can find yourself at the mercy of these people. I'm sure the questions about the car were just intended to humiliate me in the first place. He knew very well I hadn't a car and he recognised that I was the sort of person who normally would have been expected to have one. If you don't have a car these days you are a sort of second-class citizen. This is very unpleasant, particularly if one has been brought up to regard one-self as rather superior, certainly very much superior to persons such as Jones.

I did what turns out to have been a rather clever thing some time ago. The local council delivered to our house a brand new bin all silvery and shiny. Obviously they intended to take away the old one, which was undoubtedly worn-out, the next time their refuse lorry was at the house. But I didn't like to think of this magnificent new bin being filled with garbage. So I quietly rescued it and hid it in the attic. The dustmen continued to use the old bin, but in another six months or so another new bin arrived. This time I didn't dare to save it. The next day the refuse men carted away the old bin and I was forced to use the newest bin of all. I did so with a feeling almost as if I was committing some sort of violation. But of course I wasn't going to give up the bin I had rescued previously to wet tea-leaves, cinders and cabbage-stalks.

When I got home last night I found the bag of wheat on the door-step. I immediately thought of the bin in the attic. I brought it down to the cellar and emptied the bag of wheat into it. Then I had another brilliant idea. I got an old screwdriver and using it as a cold chisel cut out five holes round the bottom of the bin, just above the bottom rim. A little wheat flowed out through each of these holes on to the floor, but not very much. When you pick up what has flowed out, more flows out to take its place. Two or three rats will easily be able to feed at each hole at any one time. I have thus devised a feed hopper for my rats which will keep their food in constant supply—so long as I keep the bin full—and at the same time keep it clean. Their water supply I had already arranged with drinking bowls which they can fill themselves. I used a ball-cock from which I removed the ball. In its place I put a small platform counterbalanced by a spring. When a rat jumps on to the platform the platform will sink, and with it of course the lever of the ball-cock. The tap will open and the water flow into a little drinking trough below.

The water supply arrangement is not quite satisfactory because rats do not always get off the platform immediately there is sufficient water in the trough and it then flows over the floor. As well some of the young rats are playful and like to jump on to the platform when an older rat is drinking, with the result that the water pours down on to the drinker's head. Socrates got caught this way last week and was very cross about it. I thought he would have killed the young one at first, but he just rolled him over and gave him a few admonitory nips. The young one did not attempt to fight back. All of which shows that rats are very like human beings even in their sense of humour.

The rats have been in the cellar a fortnight now and the main snag is just the reverse of what I expected. I thought I would have difficulty in keeping the rats *in* the cellar. I can't get them to leave it. Why should they? It is warm and comfortable and there is food and water in abundance.

Last night I thought I would make them leave it. I blocked all the holes in the feed bin with bits of rolled-up newspaper and laid a thin trail of wheat up the shelves and along the plank to the grating. I thought this would make them run up the plank and out through the grating. Not a bit of it. When I came back tonight I found they had pulled the newspaper stoppers out of the bin and were feeding as usual. They hadn't bothered about the wheat on the plank or shelves. This won't do. I can't go on feeding them for ever. They'll have to go out and forage for themselves. I must think of something.

I look forward to going home in the evenings now far more than I ever did when Mother was alive. I open the front door with my latch-key and close it carefully behind me. I hang up my coat and hat. I go to the cellar-door, open it a little, and peep in. There is Socrates waiting for me on the top step. 'Out you come,' I say, and out he does come into the hall. I close the door after him. None of the other rats is allowed into the house. They have the choice of staying in the cellar or going out through the grating into the garden. They stay in the cellar. Nothing I can do will persuade them to go out. I keep buying wheat. I can't afford it, but so long as I can actually lay my hands on money I haven't the strength of mind to drive them out by starvation.

Socrates is allowed to stay in the house from the time I come in at night till the time I leave for work in the morning. In the mornings, just before I leave, I put him back through the cellar-door and he spends the day with the other rats. The rest of the time he is with me and I share everything with him, even my bed. He is perfectly clean. He is house-trained that is. I had no difficulty in training him. The first evening I let him into the house he left droppings all over the place, but each time I saw him do something I picked it up with a piece of stiff paper and put it into an old frying-pan that was in the kitchen. Very soon he saw what I was up to and by the end of the evening when he had anything to do he hopped into the frying-pan and did it there. The advantage of the frying pan is that it's so easy to carry round. From time to time I either tip it out of the window, or into the W.C. Whichever is most handy.

That first night, when bedtime came, I didn't like to put Socrates down in the cellar. It seemed mean somehow. So I got a big cardboard box that had come from the grocer's and a bit of an old blanket. I put the bit of blanket in the box, and the box on the floor of my bedroom with the frying-pan beside it in case Socrates wanted to do anything in the night. When I awoke in the morning I found he was on the bed under the quilt, pressed up close against me for warmth. Now he often comes right into bed with me. At first I was frightened that I might roll over on top of him. But he always manages to keep out of the way. On warm nights he sleeps on my pillow.

The work in the office is increasing. I don't know if the turnover has increased very much, but certainly the number of orders has. This means more work for everyone, particularly me. I had to work late three nights last week. Anyone working late in our office is entitled to half-a-crown for tea-money. So I paid myself half-a-crown each of the nights I worked late and entered the payments in the cash-book. Jones looks at the cash-book every morning. On

Friday morning he said to me, 'Is all this working late really necessary?'

I said, 'I can't keep up otherwise. There's an awful lot more to
do.'

Jones said, 'You *should* be able to keep up. It's all a matter of
efficiency. In future I want the day's work done in the day. We
can't afford to be paying out tea-money the whole time. It's not
economical.'

All he really wants is to stop me getting seven and six extra
a week. He knows very well that when I'm going to work late I
bring in sandwiches and don't actually spend any money extra in
having tea. So now I'll simply have to go on working late without
charging tea-money. Long ago when Jones was no more than one
of the men in the warehouse I heard another man say he was a
mean bastard. I don't know if he really is a bastard or not, but he
certainly is mean.

We've now got a girl in the Cash Office. She started today. Whoever heard of a girl in the Cash Office before. I'm not sure what
Jones is up to. He says she's there to help all round and lighten the
work. But with Jones you never know. Perhaps he's really come to
the conclusion that I'm inefficient or alternatively that a girl would
be cheaper. Well I don't know whether you would call me efficient.
I always thought I was pretty quick with a pen and I know I make
very few mistakes. At the same time I don't think I *look* efficient. I
mean I've somehow got to look old-fashioned. I don't know quite
why this is because you'd still call me almost a young man. I know
this—the work I send out is a lot more reliable than what comes
out of other places. If you saw the invoices that come in to us nowadays, half of them extended wrong and as for the statements. . . .
As often as not there's something on them intended for another
firm altogether. It's all these girls. They're thinking of what they
call 'Dates' the whole time. Their minds are never on their work.
And now *we've* got one. Mind you we always had girls to do the
typing, even in Father's day. But that's quite a different thing from
getting them mixed up with the work of the Cash Office.

The new girl has now settled into a regular job—she checks all

the invoices before they are allowed to go out. In the old days all
the invoices were written by the Invoice Clerk and checked by
the Despatch Clerk. Then Jones altered the system so that there
was only one clerk in the Despatch Office. But of course the new
system meant more mistakes. Whether he's got in the girl to put
this right, or with the idea of replacing me, I'm not sure. At any
rate for the first fortnight she was here she was what was called
'Being trained', which meant that she was shown all the work in
the office, particularly my work. I couldn't refuse to show her my
work when I was ordered to do so by the Book-keeper, who had
been ordered by Jones. But I didn't show her more than I could
help. I told her I hadn't time to explain things, and she'd just have
to watch. In fact I *really* didn't have time, even with working late.
She spent a week sitting beside me watching what I did. At the
end of it she said I had been very helpful. In fact she seems a very
nice girl and I would have got to like her if I hadn't kept reminding
myself the whole time that she was trying to steal my job. As it
was we became quite friendly in a superficial fashion. The last day
I said to her with a touch of irony, 'Well, I suppose you could do
my job now as well as I can, or perhaps better.'

'Goodness no!' she exclaimed. 'I just don't know how you
manage. I'd be here all night, and still not finished.'

I didn't tell her that I'm often here till eleven o'clock. She might
think then that perhaps I wasn't so much more efficient than she is
after all. As it is I think she must have told Jones and/or the Book-
keeper that I am very efficient indeed. The Book-keeper ought to
know already that I am at least moderately efficient, but perhaps
he himself feels under pressure from Jones. For all he knows he
may be the next. One of these days Jones may want to replace *him*.
Anyhow the girl has now got the regular job of checking invoices.
So the position seems to be held for the time being.

The Book-keeper told me today that Jones's real idea in getting the
girl was as a sort of insurance against a breakdown in the office
routine. If the Book-keeper gets ill, or I get ill, or the Despatch
Clerk gets ill the whole machinery of running the office is put out
of order. The girl is intended as a sort of spare cog.

I don't know whether to believe this or not. The Book-keeper has obviously swallowed it whole. Jones may even believe it himself in a sort of way. The thing about people who deceive is that their minds work in different compartments. They can have two contradictory theories in their head at once and speak according to one or the other, whichever suits the listener best. I think Jones has the idea that the whole office could be run by girls more cheaply than by men, but he's not sure yet how it would work out. So he's got this one girl as a kind of spare—just what he said to the Book-keeper in fact. He reckons one or other of us is bound to get ill some time. The girl will then be shoved in as a stop-gap. If she gets on all right the person whom she's been stop-gapping for will be due for the sack at the earliest opportunity.

I thought of mentioning this idea to the Book-keeper and suggesting that we ought all to get together and arrange that if any one of us does get ill the others will make sure that the girl is not able to carry on his work satisfactorily. I didn't dare to. The Book-keeper would be shocked. He is one of these old-fashioned persons who would cut his own throat if the Boss told him to.

I am beginning to get the odd impression that the girl likes me. As a rule girls pay very little attention to me. With their quick feminine intuition they recognise at once that I'm a bad bet, not worth wasting time on. Occasionally I've felt that a girl was sorry for me, but that was as far as it ever went.

This girl appears to respect me. She always speaks to me in a respectful way. Of course it may all be part of a deep-laid plot to get my confidence. She is always offering to help me and the way she does it you would think she meant it. She said yesterday, 'You know you've far more to do than anyone else in the office. You really should let me help you. I haven't enough to keep me occupied.' This was very tempting, because it's true. The work keeps mounting and mounting. I worked late four nights last week— Monday, Tuesday, Wednesday, Thursday. And it will be the same again this week. However I refused. I did it as nicely as possible, because I can't help liking her.

I never work late on Friday nights. The reason is that on Fridays Jones works late himself. He makes out new price-lists for the travellers. So I look forward to Fridays, and of course the week-ends.

I don't really like work. I only work hard because I'm afraid of losing my livelihood.

All the same it's not hard work in itself I object to. What I hate is losing my free time. It's so cosy at home in the evenings since Mother died. From the moment I get in and open the door of the cellar I have a feeling of complete contentment. Most of the time I spend alone with Socrates. I don't really bother much about the other rats. I see to their food and comfort of course, but I don't usually stay down in the cellar more than an hour or so even on the nights when I'm not working late. All the same their education is coming on, though of course they're not up to Socrates' standard. Socrates, I do believe, understands every word I say. I think during the day when I'm not there he must teach the other rats. For instance they can all now count up to ten, and I don't think they could do that from my teaching alone. There is one young rat that seems brighter than the others. Funnily enough he isn't as definitely a furry-tail as some. I suppose you would call him an intermediate type. I can't quite make out where he came from. I don't remember him being there when I moved the rats from the tool-shed into the cellar. Of course he might have been born in the cellar since the move, but I can't remember him as a baby rat or half-grown, and he never seemed to belong to any particular family. Somehow I feel that he is a son of Socrates, though I have no means of knowing, and I don't suppose Socrates has either. I am inclined to think he has made his own way in. I have given him the name of Solomon. It's because he's so clever, but even if the name hadn't been taken already I would never have called him Socrates.

Solomon I look on as a crafty kind of name, while Socrates is good and wise.

Most nights now I get in so late and so tired that I have only time to feed the rats and go to bed. I wish I could take Socrates into the office with me. Then I could let him out after all the others have gone to keep me company when I'm just there by myself. But it would mean keeping him shut up in a bag all day and that wouldn't be fair.

Not getting tea-money has quite upset my budget. Tea-money was sheer profit to me. I brought in a Thermos flask of tea and a few slices of bread and margarine, which was just what I would have been having at home anyhow. I suppose you might say I have enough to live on. I would have if I sold the house and took a room somewhere, which is all that a solitary bachelor is supposed to need. Now I've got my bill for rates staring me in the face. It can be paid in two instalments, but even one instalment is going to take all the money I have left in the bank, plus nearly all my month's pay. I'm going to pay it, though I'll have to wait till the end of the month. I'm out of coal too, but fortunately I've enough wheat to do for some time. I won't be the first person who's had to live on bread and water for a stretch. And the weather's hardly ever really cold before Christmas.

I've had another of my ideas. Not that it's going to make me any money. It's about bringing Socrates into the office. Next to the Ladies' cloakroom there's what we call, 'The Old Bookroom.' We used to put the old ledgers and day-books into it when they got full up, because no one liked to throw them away in case they might be needed for something. Even before Father died all the shelves were full up and there were some books on the floor. Now it's never used and no one ever even opens the door. Why not put Socrates in *there*? He could run about in perfect freedom all day without anyone being a penny the wiser, and then at night I could bring him into the Cash Office with me. I'll have a look tomorrow before I do anything.

Well I had my look and everything was even better than I imagined. The door was locked, but the key was in the lock. So I went in and had a look round. From any normal point of view the room's jammed full, but that doesn't mean there's not still plenty of room for Socrates to run about as he likes. However I wasn't going to take any chances. When I came out I locked the door and put the key in my pocket. I made sure no one saw me doing this. Now I have waited a week and no one has shown any interest in the Bookroom. If anyone does they're sure to come to me before trying to burst open the door. I'll say, 'I believe Father had a duplicate key for that at home. If you wait till tomorrow I'll have a look and bring it in if it's there.' That'll give me all the time I need to make sure Socrates is out of the way before they get in.

Thank goodness I don't owe anything. That was one thing Mother insisted on after Father died. We never ran any bills, except for electricity and gas. That way you always know where you are. With electricity and gas she worked out what they came to each quarter and put something aside each week in a special envelope. At the end of the quarter there was always a little more than enough. I did the same at first, but I wasn't using enough electricity to justify the quarterly rental charge. Now I've got them to put in slot-meters and I must say I find them very satisfactory. I never have more than one light on at a time. If that goes out and I haven't a shilling in the house I just have to do without till the next day. It's a bit awkward at times but it does save money.

Today I took Socrates into the office with me. I used Father's leather travelling bag. I slipped into the Bookroom when nobody was looking and locked the door after me. Then I opened the bag and let him out. I put out some food for him. Immediately Socrates started to explore. I watched him for a minute or so. He seemed contented enough and I decided it would be all right to leave him. I took the key out of the keyhole and peered through, listening at the same time. I could see no one and hear no one. I came out quickly and locked the door behind me. There was no one about. It was only ten past nine. The girls don't come in till half-past. After that I knew I shouldn't have another chance to see Socrates and find out how he was getting on till lunch-time.

In fact I didn't see him at lunch-time. It appears that none of the girls goes home in the middle of the day. They bring sandwiches in with them and make tea in the Ladies' room. All through the lunch-hour they were going in and out. The way our office is nowadays you never know who is watching who. I felt if I was seen going in or out of the Bookroom Jones would hear about it in no time and start asking questions.

The result of all this was that I didn't see Socrates again till everyone else had gone home. I went into the Bookroom and called him. I called and called. Soon I began to get worried. I couldn't think what to do. How far could he have gone? Might he have set off to try to get home? What sort of chance would he have through streets thronged with traffic, or later, if he did get past those first hazards, in back streets inhabited by stray cats and vicious dogs? I had nearly given up hope when I found him curled up, asleep and almost invisible, in a corner of the travelling bag.

For a moment I wondered if he was dead. It occurred to me he might have been eating the leather off the back of the old books, and that the leather might be treated in some way which made it poisonous. But there was nothing wrong with him except that he was lonely and miserable. His coat was all ruffled and dull. When I stroked him for a little his spirits returned to normal. He began to groom himself. Very soon he was sleek and shining as usual. I never noticed before what a big rat he has become. He never seems to have stopped growing.

After that I took him into the Cash Office and he ran about there quite happily for two or three hours—in fact till I was ready to go home. I don't think I'll take him into the office again. It wouldn't be kind, really.

I didn't like giving up the idea of taking Socrates to the office. I tried to think of some safe way to do it without making him miserable. I decided he had been miserable just because he was lonely and perhaps frightened at the same time. If I took in another rat as well that would stop him being lonely. If I go the proper way about it I may also be able to stop him being frightened.

For his companion I have decided on Ben Suleiman. Ben Suleiman is the rat I previously called Solomon. I don't know why I changed his name. It is almost as if he forced the new name on me.

Today is Sunday. This morning at about the time I would have been getting ready for church if Mother were still alive, I put Socrates and Ben Suleiman in the travelling bag and caught a bus into the city. The city is very quiet on Sundays. There was no one at all in the street where our office is. I always carry with me Father's key of the office. It is one thing Jones has never tried to take away from me. If he did I wouldn't be able to lock up when I work late. And if

he asked about it and didn't take it away he couldn't go on pretending not to know about my working late. So he would either have
to stop me or let me take tea-money again, and I don't think he
really wants to do either.

Anyhow I let myself in, took the two rats down to the Bookroom and released them. From time to time I went back and
peeped in. They both seemed perfectly happy.

The reason I chose Ben Suleiman is that I think he is the only
rat who is Socrates' equal intellectually. In fact I think he may
be superior even to Socrates as regards intellect. But there is still
something about him I don't like.

I went home about six. I got all my back work cleared up. I
worked all the time just as if it had been a normal day, but the
amount I got through surprised me. In the office during the day I
am kept back by constant interruptions, people wanting this and
that. At nights my rate of work is slowed down, I think, just by the
fact that I am tired. If I work an occasional Sunday in future it will
be as good as three nights and I will be able to bring in as many rats
as I can carry without fear of anyone finding out.

Jones is getting in consultants. The girl heard about them from
Jones's 'Secretary'—as he now calls the typist who does his letters.
In Jones's world a secretary is as essential to prestige as a car.

'But what *are* consultants?' I asked the girl. She and I are now
quite friendly.

'Oh they come in and discover a business is being run all wrong.
They work out economies and get in more staff to put them into
effect. They find out nobody's any good but the office boy. They
recommend he should be made managing director. Usually the firm
goes bust after that. Meantime the consultants will have moved on
somewhere else.'

'If it's like that why do people ever get them in?'

'Just it's the modern thing to do. Maybe they'll decide you and I
should be directors. That'd be fun, wouldn't it?' I realised she was
joking.

Of course it went all round the office in no time and everyone is
feeling a bit jittery. The Book-keeper said, 'You'll have to smarten
yourself up now, young man. Going to be no more inefficiency

round here.' All the older men are taking that attitude, but secretly they're scared stiff. I suppose at heart no one is really completely confident.

So far the consultants don't appear actually to have started. They just come in from time to time and have talks with Jones in private.

I don't know what to do about money. I thought again about writing to Uncle in Canada. But he never replies to letters anyway. And it might have the opposite effect to what I want. He might decide that I was shiftless and cut me out of his will—if I'm ever in it. So I just did nothing as usual.

It is only now, forty-eight hours after the event, that I can write about it any way calmly.

The night before last I was in desperation. I had only half a loaf of bread in the house and no money whatever. I could eat the bread myself and let the rats starve, or I could give them the bread and starve myself. Goodness knows we're all half-starved as it is—or were. Things have now changed, for the time being at least. As they were then I realised it didn't matter much who got the bread. We were all going to starve completely very soon. There would be no relief till the end of the month when my pittance is paid by the firm. Of course I could have robbed the till—'Borrowed a bit from the cash drawer,' is a nicer way to put it. I would have had no hesitation in doing this if I hadn't felt almost certain I would be found out. Jones has made a rule that the Book-keeper must make a surprise check on the cash at least three times a month. It's not that my cash has ever been out. I don't know if Jones even suspects me of anything. I think it's just part of the general nastiness that he calls 'Efficiency.'

As I sat there sipping a glass of cold water, and looking alternatively at the half loaf of bread and at Socrates, it occurred to me that a change had come over my moral outlook. I realised that if I could have stolen money from the firm without being found out, I would have. Nothing but fear, or prudence, kept me from being a criminal. This thought didn't make me ashamed in any way. On the contrary I felt as if a door had suddenly been opened to me.

It was as if in a game of golf I didn't need to count any more the shots which my opponent didn't see. Then it struck me that possibly Jones had discovered this a long time ago, and hungry as I was, I laughed. Socrates looked up quite frightened. I don't often laugh.

For some time I couldn't think of how to take advantage of my new discovery. All sorts of grandiose schemes for robbing banks and mail vans flitted through my mind. After fifteen minutes or so I became more practical. What I want now, I said to myself, is food for myself and the rats. Fortune can come later. All about me there is food in plenty. My neighbours have food. The shops are full of food. All I have to think of is how to get possession of some without paying.

The first thing that struck me was that if I could feed the rats I could eat the half-loaf myself. Of course only a temporary solution, but an urgent temporary solution was what I needed most. I thought immediately of Major Robinson. I don't know why. He is not quite my nearest neighbour. But he is often away and more than once I have yielded to the temptation of helping myself from his garden. It's so easy to get into, and quite a lot of what he grows never gets used in any case. It's a pity to let it go to waste.

The fact is I know Major Robinson's garden and I know the back of his house. Indeed I have sometimes peered through the larder window. . . . There are two windows really. From one the glass has been removed and replaced by a fine wire mesh that not even a midge could squirm through. But it would be quite easy to knock a hole in it. My fist would probably do the trick, and there would be no noise, as there would be if I had to break glass. I could let the rats through the hole in the wire and they could eat as much as they liked. If anyone did come, which would be unlikely if I chose my time right, what would he do if he found the larder filled with rats all eating away as fast as they could manage? Scream, if it was a woman, run for help or a stick if it was a man—and in the interval I could get the rats out of the larder and sneak quietly away. Even a brave man might hesitate to tackle forty-nine rats with a stick. Nearly everyone is a little afraid of rats. I used to be till I learned how friendly they really are. Of course Major Robinson being a military man ought to be brave, but military men nowadays think of strategy and tactics more than blind courage. Major Robinson would probably think it more correct strategically to call in the police or the fire brigade.

Before doing anything I decided to go and spy out the land. I put Socrates in one pocket of my waterproof and the half loaf of bread in the other. I was afraid, if I left it, it mightn't be there when I came back. The rats have gnawed a hole in the cellar door and though I try to persuade them to keep in the cellar I never know that I won't find them in the house.

I went straight down the road to the Robinsons'. It's built with its back to the road, and the vegetable garden is between the road and the house. There's nothing simpler than to nip in any dark night and help oneself to a cabbage, a few potatoes, or even some tomatoes out of the greenhouse. The trouble is that there hasn't been anything in the garden for the past month. Tonight it was reasonably dark and there was no light showing from the larder. I turned in at the gate without a qualm. I half-saw half-heard Nap, the Major's dog, and put out my hand to give him a pat. I've always been on friendly terms with Nap. He usually stands beside me wagging his tail when I'm taking things from the garden. But tonight he jumped up on me and began to bark in an absolute frenzy. I had quite forgotten about Socrates in my pocket, till he began to wriggle about a little.

'Down Nap! Quiet Nap!' I ordered, but it wasn't the slightest use. He is a biggish dog, a sort of mongrel Old English Sheepdog. He made no attempt to bite me, but he was determined to get Socrates out of my pocket, probably thought he was doing me a good turn. Imagined I didn't know I had a rat in my pocket. I wasn't so much afraid that he would get Socrates out. He's too clumsy for that. I was afraid that his continual jumping up might injure Socrates. I was also afraid that the noise might bring out the Major to see what was wrong.

So I gave up and began to make for home. I had to keep twisting and turning and at the same time pushing Nap off. I was terribly tempted to kick him, but I didn't want to make an enemy of him. I knew I'd want to use the garden again sometime. Then the lights went on at the back of the Robinsons' house and the next thing was the Major's authoritative, military voice. 'Nap! Nap! Come home, Sir. At once.'

'Go *home,*' I whispered, giving him a sort of half-kick. He yelped and, by a miracle, turned tail and went.

I ran for home—on tip-toes so as to make no noise.

I heard the Major and Nap meet. 'What's the matter, boy? What are you barking at? What's all the fuss?' I knew he would come strolling out to the gate to investigate.

I raced up our own drive, and in through the yard and the back door. I felt safe. I was quite sure the Major hadn't seen me. Of course even if he had, he couldn't have done anything. I've as much right to be on the road as he has. All the same he would have thought it strange, if Nap had started to jump up at me again, barking in that hysterical fashion.

Fancy calling a dog 'Napoleon', because that's what Nap's short for. The Major apparently has always been a great admirer of the Emperor, admires his strategy. . . . Bit out of date, you'd think. Maybe that's why he only got to be a Major. I mean, even in the army. . . .

I went out again in about fifteen minutes. This time I left Socrates though I still kept the lump of bread in my pocket. I didn't intend to try the Major's again, though by now Nap was probably safely shut in. That didn't say he wouldn't start barking away again like mad the moment I got near the house. But there are several other houses in our road—and then it suddenly struck me. A new grocer's shop has started up just opposite the end of our road. There's the shop in front, just a little back from the main road, and behind it there's a big store. The door between the shop and the store was open once, when I was in the shop, and I got a glimpse of what was inside. It seemed to be just crammed with stuff, mostly food. Someone told me that the man must have more money than sense, starting a shop there and carrying such a stock. But I don't know. He seems to be getting on all right.

I went down to the main road. The shop was shut, but there was a dim light shining through it. I realised it came from a little office near the back. Probably the grocer totting up his books to see how he was doing. I went round to the very back. Quite easy because there's waste ground on either side. There's only one window at the back. It has iron bars across it, no glass. I heard that he had glass in at first. But the local hooligans kept throwing stones through it and he had to give up and put bars instead. The bars are too close for a hooligan to get through, but a rat could manage comfortably. There was no light in the store.

I went back home for the rats. I put twenty-five rats in the bag I used when I went to do Jones's tyres. I carried it down and left it at the back of the grocer's store, not just under the window, but a little way off in a bunch of nettles, where even if anyone did come along it wouldn't be seen. 'Quiet,' I said. 'I'll be back.' I'd never left them like this before. I hoped it would be all right. I kept Socrates in my pocket. I didn't like to leave him in case anything went wrong. I went home and brought the rest in a suitcase.

As soon as I got to the waste ground again I opened the bag I'd left and found the rats all huddled together in the bottom. They hadn't tried to get out. Probably they were frightened. I took them all to the window, and put them in through the bars, one by one— Socrates first to show the way. 'Food,' I told them. 'Eat food.' I said that to each one of them as I placed it on the window-ledge between the bars.

I don't suppose it took more than two or three minutes to put them all in. After that I could see nothing. It was quite black inside the store. I had no idea what was going on. I wondered how long I should leave them—one hour, two hours?

I ate some of the bread, but not much, because my mouth was dry and there was no water.

I hid the bag and the suitcase in the nettles and went round to the front to look at my watch in the light from the shop. It was ten past nine. I thought I might leave them till ten past eleven. By that time I would want to go home to bed. Besides I was afraid to leave them too long in case they all got tired of eating and went to sleep.

I returned to the back and leaned against the wall under the window. I thought I was safe there. If I hung about in front someone might notice me. Not that anyone could say anything. Still you never know. After a bit I went to the front again and had another look at my watch. Twenty-five to ten. I was bored stiff. If only I could have seen the rats. All I knew was that there was an occasional rustling of paper, an occasional slight fistling noise.

I had an electric torch at home. I wished I had brought it. I thought of going back for it. It would only mean leaving the rats for ten or fifteen minutes, and it would help to put in the time.

And then something fell inside the store. It didn't make much noise. It might have been a packet of cornflakes falling from a shelf four or five feet from the ground. I wondered if the grocer would hear it and wonder. Was the door between the shop and the store open or closed? Was the door of his little glass office open or closed? I didn't know. I hesitated. Should I call the rats back quickly, before there was any chance of discovery, or was I being too jittery?

The light went on in the store. At the same time there was quite a loud noise. I don't know what sort of noise. I think it was the noise of the grocer flinging open the door. I expect he tried to open the door and switch on the light almost simultaneously, with the idea of surprising the burglars. I am sure he had no idea what sort of burglars were there.

I had to stand on tip-toes to see through the window. At first I didn't see the grocer, or any rats. I suppose my eyes were dazzled. Then I saw everything. The store was bigger than I had imagined. The grocer was standing in the doorway, quite still, with his eyes wide open. The rats were quite close to him. They were all looking at him, as surprised as he was, stopped in the middle of whatever they'd been doing. Some had been crawling over a side of bacon, some digging a hole in a cheese. Others were surrounded by a sea of cornflakes. It was wonderful how much they had done in so short a time.

The grocer slammed the door. He didn't switch off the light. What will he do now? I wondered. I called the rats. 'Socrates! All of you. Quick! Here! Out! Time to go home!' They came crowding through the bars, jostling each other, the ones at the back shoving against the ones in front. I snatched Socrates, put him in my pocket and dashed to the bunch of nettles for my bag and suitcase. I should have done that, of course, *before* I called.

I dropped the case a yard or two from the window and began to open the bag so that they could jump straight into it. There was a squeal from beneath my feet, and another. I was treading on rats. Those who had got to the window first had been pushed off the ledge by the ones behind. The ground was covered with rats. I knelt down, and began to grab them, thrusting them into the bag as quickly as I could. But I remembered to count. I couldn't even see them. I grovelled about on the ground and whenever I could feel a rat I caught it and put it in. When I had twenty-four in the bag I closed it and began on the case. There were some still on the window-ledge. I could see them peering down at me. In fact they were the only ones I *could* see. I took them last. Forty-five, forty-six, forty-seven, forty-eight. . . . There must be one missing. I got down on the ground again and began to grovel. Was one of the rats I had stood on injured, perhaps killed. Suddenly I remembered. I hadn't counted Socrates. I had them all.

Now what? Where had the grocer gone? Was he in his little office telephoning the police? No. You wouldn't telephone the police for rats. What would you do? I thought I had better investigate before I took any too precipitate action. If the grocer was out at the front, waiting for the police or the fire brigade, he would think it funny if he met me coming from behind his store carrying a suitcase in one hand and a leather travelling bag in the other.

So I investigated, first putting the case and the bag back among the nettles. The light was still on in the shop, but I could see no sign of the grocer. Was he still in the office? There was a man's hat there, but it didn't move. Perhaps he was sitting down at the telephone. The front door was open. I couldn't remember if it had been open before or not. I didn't think so. Probably he had rushed out not bothering to shut it. The rats must have frightened him. He hadn't even liked to wait to telephone. The hat must be empty, stuck on top of a filing cabinet or something.

There was an easy way to find out. Walk in. If there was someone in the hat, tell them I had noticed the door open and wanted a packet of cigarettes. How's he to know I've given up smoking? . . . and what business is it of his anyhow? If he does offer me cigarettes it's time enough to discover I've no money with me and say I'm sorry for troubling him.

So I did walk in. I searched the shop. There was no one there. The hat was empty. It was hanging on a peg as a matter of fact. But there were three bundles, each containing one hundred one-pound-notes, lying on a little table where he had been working. I took Socrates out of my pocket and put him on the table. I pointed at one of the bundles of notes, 'Eat,' I said. He took a nibble and didn't like it. 'Eat,' I said again. This time he took a little more. The bundle now had a nibbled look. 'All right,' I told him and put him back in my pocket. I looked round. No sign of the grocer coming back. I went to the door of the store and using my hand-kerchief to turn the handle opened it slightly. Oh I haven't read detective stories for nothing. I went back to the office. Still no sign of anybody. I picked up the two unnibbled bundles of notes, shoved them into my pocket (not the one where Socrates was) and ran.

A bus went by without stopping and immediately afterwards two cars. I turned my back to the road. You never know who may recognise you. Where on earth had the grocer gone? Could I trust him to stay away another few minutes. I decided to chance it. I dodged round behind the store again and picked my suitcase and bag from among the nettles. It was less chancy taking them both at once than coming back when the Fire Brigade and police might be all over the place. Fortune favours the bold. I got home without meeting a soul.

Knowing that I am a criminal is like waking up and finding myself a millionaire. The main difference is that most millionaires don't mind who knows they are millionaires. I can't let anyone know I'm a criminal.

For the first time since I made friends with the rats I see clearly what I ought to do. I was like someone with a business—plant, machinery, and so on—but no working capital. Now I *have* work-ing capital—two hundred pounds. Not very much, but enough, I think, to start me.

Of course I will have to lay my plans very carefully. I will require to make the best possible use of my assets. My chief assets are my money, my house and the rats. Previously I let the little money I had fritter away. That was because I didn't think of becoming a criminal. This time I intend my money to start earning for me almost immediately. I will commit more crimes, crimes designed solely to earn money. I won't rob any more grocery stores. To keep the rats well fed I would have to rob a food store every day. Very soon we would be found out. Ideally I would like to rob a bank, but so would every criminal. Perhaps I shall rob a bank even-

tually but to begin with I must attempt something easier. I think I
know what.

This evening I bought a car. A van would have suited my purpose
better, but everyone would ask, 'What on earth does he want with
a van?' The car itself cost £50, but by the time I have paid tax and
insurance there'll be about £80 down the drain. Never mind. I hope
I'll soon get it back and a lot more with it.

The story of my raid on the grocery store has broken at last, as the
newspapermen say. They are a bit guarded about it, don't even say
where it happened. The grocer obviously doesn't want anyone to
know there were rats in his store. It looks as if he didn't report
what happened till a day or two after the event. Why he did then,
I don't know. Perhaps it leaked out. I wonder too where he ran that
night. He must have been scared out of his wits. The police anyhow are taking the matter seriously. Members of the public are
asked to report immediately to their nearest police station any
damage by rats or any sightings of rats, particularly five or more
rats moving together as if travelling with a common purpose. I
wonder who thought out that one.

 Well I don't intend anyone to see my rats. When they travel
they shall travel by car. That's what I got it for.

Curse! Curse! Curse! I am going to have to take a driving test. I
brought the car into business this morning and parked it in the yard
behind the office. I did it because I needed more wheat and meant
to get it at lunch-time. Of course I quite liked the idea of the rest
of the staff seeing that I *had* a car. Everyone went out to look at it,
particularly the Book-keeper, who of course knows my salary, and
incidentally doesn't run a car himself. 'Very nice,' he said, 'if you
can afford it. I hear these older cars take a lot to keep up.'

 'Oh I think I'll be able to manage all right,' I responded nonchalantly. 'I've got my mother's affairs pretty well fixed up at last.'
That put him in his place, not unkindly. I was what you might
call slightly superior in my manner. Perhaps he remembered. . . .
I mean that Father used to own the business, and that he was just
the Book-keeper then, as he is now.

I didn't see Jones look at my car, but I knew he would, and that he would speak to me about it. He came into the Cash Office on some pretence or other and then said, as if by chance, 'I see you've bought yourself a car.'

'Yes,' I answered. 'A car comes in very useful from time to time.'

'Where'd you get the money?' he asked. Just like that. No preliminaries. No gentle probing round.

Of course I should have told him to mind his own business. I might even have said something stronger. But I didn't. I couldn't help answering in a sort of guilty way, 'Oh I've got Mother's affairs pretty well settled up at last.'

'I didn't think she left anything.'

'Oh it's not quite as bad as that,' I told him, managing to get back a little of the nonchalant manner I had used so effectively with the Book-keeper. 'We're not quite destitute, you know.'

That flummoxed him. He didn't know what to make of me. But the cheek of the man. No boss could speak to a labourer the way some of them speak to their office staff. Either they'd get hit, or there'd be strikes right and left.

I think Jones is one of those people, who always feel that someone is doing them. Probably, if the truth were known, he did Father at some time or other, or else did us after Father died.

He went out after this little exchange and I was alternately hot and cold as I thought about it. The cheek of him asking where I'd got the money. I mean what right has he to ask questions about *my* affairs? And then afterwards, the lightness of touch with which I handled him.

But he scored in the end, damn him. He came back. 'I suppose you've a licence to drive that old jalopy of yours,' he said, with a sort of malicious twist about the end of his nose.

'Licence,' I replied. 'Of course I've had it taxed and insured.'

'I'm not talking of that. Did nobody ever tell you that you need a driving licence to drive a car?'

'Of course I've got a licence.' And of course I have, but it hasn't been renewed since before Father died. How could I forget such a thing? He noticed the uncertainty in my voice.

'You'll have to take a test,' he told me, 'and you'd better not take that car out of the yard till you've passed it.'

'I'm perfectly capable of driving,' I declared. 'I'm a very good driver.'

Jones is right. My driving licence has been out of date so long that I have to take a driving test before I'm allowed a new one. All the same I took a chance and drove the car home again that night.

The Consultant (There is only one who actually does anything.) is hard at work. The senior members of staff have been out to dinner one at a time. In the relaxing atmosphere of a restaurant, over a bottle of wine, they are supposed to bare their souls to the Consultant. The Consultant tries to discover if they're progressive, dynamic and I don't know what else. The Book-keeper is a teetotaller and wouldn't have any wine. So the Consultant drank it all. The Book-keeper isn't sure whether this will count against him or not. He thinks the Consultant is an alcoholic.

I don't count as a senior member of staff though I've been in the firm longer than nearly anyone else, except the Book-keeper, Jones, and one of the travellers. So I wasn't asked out to dinner. Instead the Consultant interviewed me in what we call 'The spare office.' It's the one the auditors use when they come in to do the books.

First I was told the Consultant wanted me. He has become sort of second boss in the place. If he wants you, you go. When I went in he was bending over his papers, too busy to look up. 'Sit down,' he said, still fistling through the bumf.

I sat down. Of course I knew it was all an act, like a young dentist keeping you waiting though you know jolly well he has no other patients. At last he looked up with a sort of Judas smile. 'I want you to relax. Anything you say will be strictly between you and me. You are free to tell me what you like about anyone in the place, Mr. Jones, any of the people who are over you, what you think of the way the place is run, any improvements you would like to suggest. Anything you say I will treat as completely confidential. You needn't have any fears on that point.' The smile was getting a bit tired looking by this time. However he kept it up. 'First of all I want you to tell me about yourself.'

Well of course I didn't mean to tell him anything. I was outraged at the nerve of the man. What right has he to come prying into my private affairs? I'm sure my father would never have allowed such a thing. But what could I do? If he told Jones I wouldn't co-operate, then where'd I be? So he probed and probed and probed and got all my background out of me. Next he wanted to know was I content in my job. I told him I was, which was a lie. Only what could I say? If I said I wasn't, he'd tell Jones (I didn't have any faith in that cock-and-bull story about it all being confidential). Jones would say, 'If you don't like the job, you needn't have it. Goodbye.' But what I should have said was that I was content with the job as a step to higher things, because the next question he asked me was, 'Have you no fire in your belly?'

I said I didn't think so. I didn't know what he meant. Afterwards I asked the girl. She says it's something all these executive types are supposed to have nowadays. It's more or less the same as being dynamic, which is another thing you're supposed to be, and of course relaxed. She says she's sure the Consultant thinks he has fire in his own belly, but it's probably just wind. The girl likes making jokes that aren't quite proper. I haven't laughed so much for years as I have since she came to the office. All the same she agrees that the questions the Consultant asked me are quite ridiculous. I mean there ought to be a law against it. Everyone is entitled to a certain amount of privacy.

My life of crime is temporarily postponed. Of course I can drive a car perfectly well and there is really no reason why I should have to take a test, but it appears the Highway Code has been altered in the last few years and that I will be expected to answer questions on it. I have therefore enrolled myself as a pupil in a driving school. I find this a little humiliating, but to fail my test would be even more so. My instructor admits that I can drive a car, but says that my road sense needs brushing up. He also says that I must study the Highway Code as if it was The Catechism and I a candidate for Confirmation. I'm quite sure that the driving school just wants to make money out of me and that even if I were Stirling Moss they would make some excuse to give me lessons.

After all I am not losing much time. Though I can't take the car out on the road I am getting the rats accustomed to it in the garage. I

am training them to go in and out through the boot. I've made a
sort of wedge contrivance, partly wood partly wire, which holds
the lid of the boot just wide enough open for the rats to get in and
out. And I've two boards for them to run up and down. The ends
of the boards clip on to the edge of the boot so that there's no
danger of them slipping off while the rats are using them. I'm not
going to be able to make many raids before the police guess what
is happening and start to take precautions. I will need to try to get
hold of a few fairly big sums of money and then stop for a long
time to let people's suspicions die down.

At the moment I'm quite well off. Taking my salary into account
I've enough to last me six months or a year, living rather more
comfortably than I have recently—say more or less up to the same
standard as before Mother died.

I am by nature a cautious, even timid, individual. To undertake any
hazardous adventure is foreign to my nature. All I would like is to
lead a quiet peaceful life, bothering no one and being bothered by
no one. But Destiny it seems wills otherwise. In other words I have
not been able to think of any easy way, even making the fullest use
of my mastery over the rats, of laying my hands on large sums of
money without incurring considerable risks. Whatever I eventually do I shall take all possible precautions. In any case there is no
need to act precipitately. I have plenty of time to plan.

I realise now how fortunate I was in my raid on the grocer's.
Where can I find someone like him, someone perhaps even more
timid than myself, counting over large sums of money alone, late
at night, and ready to run a mile at the sight of a few rats? Yet
something like that is what I've got to find.

Yesterday I yielded to a sudden temptation and took the girl out for
a run in the car. I don't quite know why I did it, but now of course
I wish I hadn't. I suppose there were a number of reasons. I'd got
my driving test, and she congratulated me. I said it was simply a
matter of form. I'd been able to drive perfectly well all along. Then
I didn't want her to think I was just blowing. So I thought I'd better
show her. Of course I like her. And I did want to show someone
the car. I think I got quite a bargain.

I only meant to take her quite a short run, but as soon as we got into the car I said (absolutely foolishly), 'Where would you like to go?'

'I'd like to see where you live. Why not drive out *there*?'

'There's nothing to see.' I wanted to put her off gently, but she's very persistent.

'I'm sure there's plenty to see. We were past in the car, with Daddy, the other Sunday and it looked very interesting. Of course you can see nothing from the road, but I'm sure it's lovely inside.'

It's extraordinary how quickly a feeling of tenderness almost can change to absolute hate. 'So that's what you're after,' I thought to myself. 'You're just like all the rest of them. But if you think you're going to see inside *our* house, you've made one big mistake.' Funny the way I still think of it as *our* house, meaning Father, Mother and me. Aloud, of course I didn't say anything. Not just then. If I'd taken her home, given her a push down the cellar steps, and bolted the door after her, she'd have got a queer surprise. Still without a word I started the engine and drove off.

'But this isn't the right way,' she remarked after a minute or two.

'It's the way we're going,' I answered. That kept her quiet for a bit.

We drove into the country and presently I forgot how angry I was. She began to chat away about the office and the other people who work there. She's noticed all sorts of things about them that I would never have thought of. In this way the miles and the time went by without my very much realising. Suddenly she put up her hand and yawned. 'Do you know, I could eat a horse,' she said.

It hadn't occurred to me that she might expect me to feed her. 'My goodness!' I exclaimed. 'I didn't notice the time. Will your people not be wondering what's happened to you?'

'Oh no,' she replied. 'I gave them a ring before we left the office. I told them I was coming out with you and wouldn't be back for tea.'

This fairly took the wind from my sails. I'd never meant to ask her out for tea. We were coming into a village at the time and the first thing I saw was a big roadhouse with a lot of posh cars parked outside it. Perhaps that was what she'd been thinking of, but I pretended not to notice. I went on till we came to one of these places 'Teas with Hovis'. Even so it was horribly expensive.

I was upset going home. Never again, I kept telling myself. Never again. You'd have thought she might have had the sense to realise I wasn't feeling exactly chummy any more, but not a bit of her. She got on about the house again. 'Do let me see it,' she begged. 'Go on. Be a dear.'

I managed to keep my manners. Probably it would have been better if I hadn't. 'It's a fearful mess,' I told her. 'I couldn't possibly show it to you.'

She gave a little laugh. 'Oh I know what men are like. Mummy and I went away once, just for the week-end, and left Daddy and the boys. You would hardly believe the mess they got the house into. Just in one week-end. Every knife, fork, spoon and plate in the house was piled in the kitchen sink or round it, and not one single thing had been washed.'

'Maybe our house is worse than that.'

'Then I'd love to come in some night and wash up for you. I really would, and I could make your tea for you as well. I'm sure you never make yourself proper meals. Do you now?'

'My meals are all right.'

'But I'd love to. I really would.'

I'm sure she would—until she saw the rats. And that wouldn't be very long. I wondered what she'd make of old Socrates. Probably go screaming out of the house like a scalded cat. And then the fat'd be in the fire. The next thing the sanitary people would be out and the vermin destruction squad. No thank you.

I dumped her at her own house. She never even guessed there was anything wrong. I think she thought I would like to kiss her. Put up her face sort of way before she got out of the car. I thought if I'd given her nose a good bite that might have cooled her ardour. I didn't even get out of the car. I just suddenly let in the clutch, whizz, and left her standing in the middle of the road.

It was quite late and I couldn't help thinking of poor old Socrates waiting patiently for his supper, wondering, very likely, what had become of me.

At half-past two this afternoon Jones sent for me. He was just in

from his lunch and by the smell when he spoke I think he must
have had a drink or two. I couldn't imagine what he wanted, but
naturally I felt nervous. It's always a little frightening to be told
that the Boss wants to see you. Specially when you don't like the
Boss very much and think he doesn't like you.

Jones was grinning away, all over himself with gush. I wonder
was he nervous. 'Sit down,' he said. 'Sit down and make yourself
comfortable.'

I sat down distrustfully. What's he up to now I wondered. Is
he going to have another go at getting the house or has the Consultant recommended that my salary should be raised. (Ha-Ha.)

'Of course you know I always had great respect for your father,'
Jones began. 'Great respect. A very fine man. The type of man you
rarely find nowadays.'

I nodded my head. I couldn't think what he was at. Surely he
hadn't called me in just to tell me what a fine man Father was.

Jones started again. 'On account of you being your father's son
we've always tried to give you special consideration.'

Another long pause. Once more I nodded my head vaguely to
show I understood. Who is 'We,' I wondered. It's not surprising
royalty get muddled if someone so far down the scale as Jones can
call himself 'We.'

'We would have liked to think that there was always room in
the firm for a son of your father, but to be frank we've been disappointed in you.'

Suddenly I realised that he was going to sack me. For a moment
I felt quite numb with shock. Then I realised that I must argue with
him, plead with him to keep me on. 'But, but . . .' I mumbled halt-
ingly. 'I mean I didn't know there'd been anything wrong with my
work. I mean, I haven't been making mistakes or anything have
I?'

'Tch-tch,' he said crossly. 'It's not your work. It's your capabili-
ties. We can't afford to go on paying a man to do a girl's work, and
you're not fit for any more responsible position.'

'But how do you know?' I demanded, bold with desperation.
'I've never been given a chance at anything else.'

'You've been given every chance,' he replied. 'I understand your
potential is rated as nil.' He turned over some papers and looked

secretly at one of them. 'Yes. "Potential Nil."' Obviously this was the work of the Consultant.

I had to keep on talking. If I kept on talking I might somehow be able to stay in my job. I wouldn't be sacked till he actually told me so. He wanted to tell me, but he was having difficulty. I must have something about me. He feels that I am still the real boss's son, and he's frightened to sack me. Or perhaps it's because I'm the boss's son he wants to sack me. Much more likely. All these thoughts flashed through my mind. I said, 'You mean there's no other job in the firm that you feel you could promote me to?'

'Exactly.' You could see that he got pleasure from using a word like that. It made him feel so competent. A man of decision, he thought to himself. A man of few words.

'But I'm doing my present job all right.' I knew he couldn't deny that.

'You're doing your present job reasonably enough,' he admitted in a lofty way, 'but it's a job you've been doing since you came out of your apprenticeship. We can't go on paying a man to do work that could be done equally well by a girl, or a boy just into the place a year or two.'

'But I'm not paid as much as the men in the store,' I pointed out. 'I haven't had a rise since before Father died and all other wages have gone up lots of times.'

'We could get a girl to do it for less money,' he said. 'We'd have liked to keep you, on your father's account, but there's no room for sentiment in business nowadays. Everything has to be stream-lined, cut to the bone. Can't afford an extra penny anywhere.'

I saw a glimmer of hope. 'If it's just a matter of salary. . . . I mean if you really would keep me on Father's account. I mean I could maybe take a bit of a reduction.'

'This is very awkward,' he grumbled. 'We'd decided to have your job done by a girl. In fact there was one coming to see me this afternoon. Now what am I going to do?' He put on a worried expression.

'If you could see your way to keep me I'd do the job for what-ever you were going to give *her.*'

'That's all very well,' he said, 'but we don't want you coming back in six months' time, and asking for a rise. If you're going to stay you'll have to take what we give you, and be thankful.'

'If you let me stay I won't ask for a rise again. I'll leave it to you to give me what you think fit.'

'I'll think it over,' he said, suddenly becoming just himself in the singular. 'Now you'd better get back to your work and not waste any more of my time.'

I sneaked out. I went back to my desk in the Cash Office. I sat down, but I couldn't work. I felt covered in shame. So they didn't want me any more. They thought a girl could do the work as well—and at less money. After all these years they'd just throw me on the street. My father's old firm too. I hated Jones and his efficiency.

After a while I got out of my daze a bit. People came in and I had to attend to them. Maybe I wouldn't get the sack. Maybe he'd let me stay on with a bit of a cut in salary. And no one need ever know. It wouldn't make all that difference. I hadn't been able to manage before on what I was getting. I'd just have to speed up the start of my criminal activities.

Presently the girl came along. There was no one in the Cash Office now, but the two of us. She put her hand on my shoulder and leaned over me. I was conscious that she was female and attractive. Ordinarily I would have resisted such feelings, having long ago realised that they only lead to complications. But today I felt weak. I pressed my cheek against her arm. 'What's the matter?' she asked.

'Nothing much. Just Jones being his usual charming self.'

'What's he up to now?'

'Oh apparently I'm unnecessary. The job could be done as well and more cheaply by a girl.'

Why did I tell her this? I hadn't meant to tell anyone. I didn't know what had come over me. I realised presently that her left hand had moved from my right shoulder to my left cheek. Her right hand was on my right wrist. She was pressing my face into herself. I felt what I suppose must have been a kiss on the top of my head. I had an extraordinary sensation of comfort. All my troubles seemed to be wiped out. A feeling of bliss and peace. 'You poor, poor man,' she murmured, kissing me again.

Suddenly she drew away. The Book-keeper was returning. He

came in, and looked at me—rather oddly, I thought. But I don't think he can have seen anything. I mean me and the girl.

Time passed. The girl went off to the Ladies to help with the afternoon tea-making. Later she came back with a cup for me and one for the Book-keeper. I noticed that I had been given a saucer. This was a special attention. Usually only Jones and the Book-keeper get saucers. The girl went back to the Ladies to have her tea with the other girls. Seems a funny place to have it when you come to think of it, but they've always done it that way.

The girl came back and the Book-keeper was sent for by Jones. He stayed quite a while. I wondered if they were discussing me—whether I should be kept or not. I said to the girl, 'I wonder if they're talking about me.'

She looked puzzled. 'You mean Mr. Jones. . . .'

I gave a sort of little laugh. 'Well both of them. It takes two to make a conversation.'

'You mean Mr. Jones is telling him that he's, he's. . . .' She looked embarrassed and then came out with it. 'That he's given you the sack.'

I shrugged my shoulders. 'I'm hoping that he's telling him just the opposite, that . . .'

She interrupted and of course failed to take in what I was saying. 'I'm sure he must have told him beforehand.'

'In that case he may be telling him that he's changed his mind. I hope so.'

'But do you think he *will* change his mind?'

'I don't see why not. He said he'd think it over.'

'Think what over?'

'My proposition.'

Suddenly she got quite cross. 'What proposition? I don't know what you're talking about.'

'I suggested that he should keep me on.'

'You *did?* But what makes you think he'll pay any attention?'

'I offered very favourable terms.'

'I don't understand.'

'I said I'd take less money. Whatever the female replacement was to get, I'd take the same. Complete equality of the sexes.'

'Oh you fool,' she exclaimed. 'You bloody, bloody fool.'

I was quite surprised at her language. 'I don't see there's any sense calling names,' I told her.

'But don't you see, that's what he meant you to do. It was a trap and you walked straight into it. He'd no intention of sacking you. He just worked out this little scheme to get you to take less money.'

'Nonsense. I don't believe a word of it.'

And I don't. I'm not sure I wouldn't believe Jones's word rather than hers. Specially after what I've thought of since. Jones said there was a girl coming in to see him this afternoon about my job. See above. But no girl came. At least no girl from outside came. The only girl he saw was *her*. When she brought in his tea. He'd been going to tell her then and she'd some idea of it. When he didn't she didn't worry, because I'd already told her I was getting the sack. She thought everything was going smoothly from her point of view. That explains why she was so cross when I told her I might be staying on. Just shows. You can never trust a woman. Not that I did trust her. But just think. Kissing me and all that.

Today Jones sent for me again. It was like him to keep me on tenterhooks for a week. He's a sadist. I'm to stay on, but it's to be the way he said. I'm never to ask for a rise again. I'm to accept what they give me and be thankful. I promised. I'm being cut three pounds a week. I promised that I wouldn't let it make any difference, that I'd still work as hard as I possibly could in the best interests of the firm. So I will, but I'll get even with him yet, somehow.

Some pal of Jones's is going for a week to London and then doing a tour of the continent. Taking the wife. A second honeymoon, Jones calls it. Jones is green with envy. It's not that he wants to go to the continent himself, or even London for that matter. It's just he's appalled that someone he knows can be in a position to spend so much money. For half-an-hour today he was with the Bookkeeper, trying to work out what the whole trip will cost. Jones of course only understands one side of the business of money. Money for him is something you acquire and endeavour to keep. Every penny he makes is a pennyworth more of success. Every penny he spends is a pennyworth of failure. Perhaps that's not altogether true. He wants a bit of show as well. He wants our house. I don't think he'll ever feel he's really Boss till he gets it. Probably he plans to get it so cheap that it won't cost him any more than the house he's in. Besides he probably reckons that a house is just money in another form—so that buying a house isn't really spending. But to spend a thousand pounds—and that's what the Book-keeper says the trip will cost—and come back with nothing solid to show for it. . . . I should like to tell him that I know people who go to the continent every year, but of course I can't. I'm not included in the conversation. It's the Robinsons. Not that I know them very well. It would be funny if the Joneses had to start keeping up with the Robinsons.

I told the girl my joke about the Joneses keeping up with the Robinsons. I suppose it's not much of a joke, but it made her laugh. I like making her laugh. It makes me feel happy. She always smiles when she says 'Good morning.' I suppose she smiles the same way to everyone—or at least to everyone she's friendly with—but somehow I always feel it's a special smile for me. I find myself looking forward to it from the time I wake up in the morning. I actually like going into the office.

I don't think she really can have been trying to take my job, though maybe Jones meant to give it to her. I wish I'd never even thought that against her.

Jones was in great excitement again today about his friends the second honeymooners. They're actually taking £150 in notes for the London part of their trip plus an undisclosed sum in travellers' cheques for the continent. Mr. Honeymooner is to go to the bank on Monday to collect. They start off first thing on Tuesday. I pricked up my ears—£150 in notes. Just the opportunity I'd been waiting for. I couldn't afford to let it slip. £150 would do me for a long time. It would make up for the cut in my salary for a whole year.

'Who are these people?' I asked the Book-keeper, as soon as Jones was gone.

'A couple called Malcomson. His father left him a bit of property near the centre. There was an old clothes shop with a big yard behind it. It used to be used as a depot by some of the carriers from the country. He wasn't getting a hundred a year for it before the war. In fact for years he was getting nothing at all, because it was lying vacant and no one would take it. Now it's all part of the new development. They say he got ninety thousand from the developers. That's how it happens these days and the lucky ones can afford to go off to the continent to celebrate.'

'Very nice too,' the girl said. 'I wish someone would drop ninety thousand into my lap.'

'You wouldn't know what to do with it,' the Book-keeper told her.

'Oh yes I would,' she said. 'I'd marry someone with a hundred thousand. Money goes to money, you know.' At the same time she gave me a sly little look to indicate that she'd really marry me if she got ninety thousand. I'm quite sure she wouldn't. She'd do just as she says—go all out for some chap with a hundred thousand, or more if she could manage it. They're all the same. The biological urge plus a well-lined nest.

'Did you hear Mr. Jones's little joke?' The Book-keeper's voice showed respect for Jones, but at the same time reserved the right to be patronising about the joke. He let us know that it wouldn't be a very good joke and that he feels as superior about Jones's jokes as we do, without in any way being indiscreet.

We simpered expectantly.

'It seems the Malcomsons lived opposite Mr. Jones for about a year after they first got the money, in a house called, "Mon Repos". Now they've moved a mile or so further out to a big place called "Sandalmount". Mr. Jones says they didn't repose in "Mon Repos" very long.'

We couldn't have believed it. Jones in excelsis. We roared. All the same I've now got the address. I shouldn't have much difficulty finding it.

I've just come back from reconnoitring Sandalmount. The house itself isn't very large, about the same size as ours. But there are a lot of grounds round it, masses of rhododendrons with rustic walks going down the side of a glen to a stream with a little wooden footbridge over it. It's the sort of place I wouldn't mind having myself. The house is at the top of the glen, very quiet, very shut off. There's not another house within half-a-mile. All of which suits me admirably.

I parked the car in the road and walked boldly in the front gate. I'd no rats with me, not even Socrates. There's this long avenue. I walked and walked under wet, dripping trees. I thought I'd never come to the end of it. At last it opened out and there was the house with lawns round it and a small kitchen garden at the back. I dodged in among the trees and worked right round the house without coming into the open. Eventually I decided that it would be safe enough to go even closer. There was no one coming in or out, or standing at the windows. Television was on in one of the downstairs rooms.

I had three problems to consider—

1) how to get the rats into the house,

2) how to get myself into the house,

3) how to get us all away safely, without danger of discovery afterwards.

I came out of the shrubberies and on to the lawn. I kept as much in the shadows as possible. I avoided walking on the paths. I didn't want to crunch the gravel. The daylight had gone, but it wasn't very dark. The stars and the lights from the house showed all I needed to see. I noticed a good many upstairs windows partly open. I felt sure they would be left open all night. There was a pile of painters' ladders behind the garage. Evidently the house was to be painted while the owners were away.

My reconnaissance was complete. I knew exactly what I intended to do. Then a whim came to me. I thought I would like to look at my victims. There they were, a couple about my own age, sitting side by side on a settee, watching the television—and the dog asleep on a rug on the floor. Very touching and domestic. Pots of money, but no little ones. Sad. The great tragedy of their lives. All their affection lavished on the dog.

I looked at the dog distrustfully. I don't mind dogs really. In fact before I became involved with rats I used to be fond of dogs. Now of course, as a criminal, I am on the other side of the fence from dogs and policemen. Dogs are the *unpaid* thugs of the Capitalists. At least dogs like that are. And come to think of it they're not unpaid at all. They live on the fat of the land. This all as I contemplated the dog's excessive belly. (Note, added later. Little did I realise the cruel fate intended for the poor creature, or that I should be the means of saving him.)

The dog turned over, sat up, yawned—and suddenly saw me. He shot across the room in a frenzy of barking. I dropped down below the level of the window. The window was open at the top and I could hear the voices of the man and his wife. 'What's all that about?' The man sounded mildly cross.

'He's been uneasy all evening. I think he's maybe worried. Poor Toby.'

'How would he be worried? He couldn't know anything about it.'

'You don't know what dogs know. They've a sixth sense.'

'Better let him out. Probably thinks there's something there.'

I ran swiftly for the trees, keeping close to the house till I was well out of the line of the window. A moment later the front door opened and Toby came tearing across the lawn after me. But by this time I was safely out of sight.

Toby came to the edge of the trees and stopped. I saw at once that he wasn't a very brave dog. He did a bit more barking and then began to sniff. 'Rats,' he said to himself, and came cautiously in my direction. I had been standing quite still behind some bushes, but obviously he was now going to find me. It was no good waiting any longer. I turned my back on him and walked quickly towards the drive. Next moment he was barking close behind me. I knew he wouldn't attack immediately. I didn't really think he would attack at all, but there was a chance that if I did nothing he would bark himself into a sufficient frenzy to snap at my legs. I didn't want a nip in the leg, or worse still in the posterior. What would I say in the office if I had difficulty in sitting down—that I'd a boil on my bum. I suppose so. The girl would be all sympathy, but she couldn't ask to see it. Anyhow I turned round suddenly and made a rush at him. He was terrified. He could hardly put himself into reverse quick enough. He almost choked in the middle of a bark. I picked up a bit of broken branch and made a slash at him. I didn't hit him, but he must have heard the swish of it through the air. He let out a shriek as if I had been skinning him alive. I saw no more of him.

I stepped down into the drive. I was out of sight of the house. I walked down towards the gate not hurrying unduly. Anyone coming in and meeting me would have thought I had just been paying a call—at the house I mean, not behind a tree, though I suppose they might have thought that too. At any rate it was quite dark, specially under the trees, and there wasn't a chance that anyone *could* have recognised me. More likely that someone might spot the number of my car parked on the roadside, but what of it? There are lots of cars parked at the roadside and it's only when you actually look in and say would they mind telling you the way back to town that the heads pop up.

But I met no one. I drove home pondering my plans. I went down to the cellar and made sure that the rats were comfortable. 'I'm sorry I've no time to talk to you now,' I told them. 'Great events are afoot.'

By this time my plans were complete. I went upstairs and sat down in my armchair in front of the fire to put down my notes on paper. Socrates jumped on my knee and I used him as a sort of bookrest. So now I am writing this, comfortable and cosy after my adventures. Tomorrow night at this time I shall be just setting forth on the much more perilous task of actually stealing the money. Shall I return safe and sound, or shall I find myself a prisoner in the hands of the police?

I left home at half-past ten and reached the Malcomsons' just before eleven. I drove straight in the gate and then backed the car up a side avenue where it was well hidden by rhododendrons. You couldn't have seen it at all from the main avenue, but I parked it so that if I had to make a quick getaway all I'd have to do was jump in and drive. I had all the rats with me—all the furry-tails that is. Since I moved the furry-tails into the house I've had nothing to do with the others.

First I had to find out what was happening at the house. I didn't expect to be able to start work for another hour or two. They might easily stay up late packing, or doing last minute jobs. On the other hand they might go to bed early so as to be fresh for the start of their holiday. I was only slightly worried about Toby. If he was there he might kick up a row and spoil everything. But I was almost certain he wouldn't be there. The Malcomsons were bound to have put him into a boarding kennel or left him with friends. They wouldn't have time to dispose of him in the morning.

I left the rats in the car and went on up through the trees towards the house. There was a light on in the hall, but all the rest of the downstairs part was in darkness. Upstairs there were lights in most of the windows. For a while I watched from a clump of bushes quite close to the house. I caught a glimpse of Malcomson and then his wife in the same room. I wondered what they were doing—packing, going to bed . . . ? Presently Malcomson came right up to one of the windows and opened it. He was in pyjamas. He stood there looking out. 'It's very warm,' he said.

'You'll catch cold if you're not careful,' a female voice answered. 'We don't want that.'

'Oh I don't think so.'

'Come to bed anyhow.' She gave a little giggle. It was so quiet. I could hear everything. He turned round and disappeared. I waited for the light to go out, but it didn't. I wondered what on earth they were doing. And then it occurred to me that they might be one of these couples who read in bed before they go to sleep. They might read for hours and I wouldn't know if they were awake or asleep. And fancy going to bed and leaving half the lights on, or did they mean to get up again and turn them off? Whichever way you looked at it they were being very extravagant.

I stepped out on to the lawn, but still kept in the shadows. I went round to the back of the house. It was quite dark there except for one window upstairs which looked like a landing window or the window at the end of a passage. I deliberately trod on the gravel once or twice on the far side from the bedroom window. Surely if Toby was any good at all he would hear and bark—but I didn't want the Malcomsons to hear. There was no bark. I went right round the house, keeping on the grass where I could, tip-toeing when I couldn't. Not a sound—except from the bedroom window, where I paused a little to listen. She seemed to be an awfully giggly woman.

I had avoided going really close to the house at the very front, because it was nearly all gravel there. Now I did so, and immediately discovered a strange thing. The outer front door wasn't shut.

There was an inner front door with a glass panel in it. This was closed. But was it locked? I tip-toed into the porch. Surely Toby must bark now if he was there. Very, very slowly I turned the door-handle, and pushed. . . . The door wasn't locked. It opened with a slight creak. I waited again, with my hand on the handle. If Toby was there at all he must bark now. But Toby wasn't there.

I laughed to myself, soundlessly. Fancy going to bed leaving the front door open and half the lights on. I had made careful and elaborate plans for getting into the house, but they wouldn't be necessary. All I'd have to do would be to walk in the front door bringing the rats with me. But not yet. I wanted to wait till the Malcomsons seemed to be asleep. I shut the door as carefully as I had opened it and went out again on to the lawn.

The bedroom light was still on. Maybe they kept it on all night. Maybe one or both of them was frightened of the dark. But no. Almost immediately the bedroom light went out. The other lights remained on. I went back to the car. By the time I came back Mr. and Mrs. Malcomson should be asleep. But even if they were suffering from insomnia I didn't think it would matter very much.

The car was parked about sixty yards from the house. Sixty yards is a very long journey for a rat, moving under its own steam. I imagine rats must be great hitch-hikers. Otherwise I don't see how they could have got round the world the way they have. My original intention had been to carry the rats up to the house ten at a time. It would have been a slow business.

Now I made a daring, perhaps rash, change of plan. I got into the car and drove it right up to the house. I didn't leave it at the front door. I didn't want the Malcomsons to see it when they came rushing out, tearing their hair and screaming. I parked it round at the back, again facing outwards, so that I shouldn't have to turn it after I came back.

I got out quickly and ran back on tip-toe to below the bedroom window. The light was on. I heard voices. 'It sounded like a car.'

'I never heard a thing.' This from Hubby.

'That's because you always keep your head under the clothes. You never hear anything.'

'I hear the beastly dawn chorus every morning.'

'I'm sure it was a car.'

'Well maybe someone made a mistake and went away again.'

'I didn't hear them go away.'

I began to regret my rashness. Then Hubby said, 'Oh well if it *is* a burglar we're well insured, and he can't get in *here*.'

'I suppose not.' Wifey evidently was a kindly soul. I thought she might have sent Hubby down to investigate, but he had her well trained. Any investigating to be done she'd obviously have to do herself, and she didn't feel like it.

'Good night, darling.' Hubby sounded quite firm.

'Good night, dearest.' And at the same moment the light went out again.

I hurried back to the car and opened the boot. The rats came pouring out. With Socrates leading the way and Ben acting as a sort of sergeant-major I walked slowly to the house. The rats followed. I put on rubber gloves and opened the front door quietly. Almost immediately I found my first objective—the telephone. I took two pieces of sticky tape from my pocket. I had cut them to the right length before leaving home. I lifted the receiver and stuck down the two small plungers with the tape. I replaced the receiver.

The rats, led by Socrates, were already at the foot of the stairs. I lifted Socrates on to the first step and went up two or three steps further myself. Socrates scrambled on to the second step, and then looked round for the rest. The rest were hesitating. They didn't seem to want to go upstairs. Ben came hustling up snapping his jaws. I fancy he distributed two or three sharp nips. The rats began to hop up the stairs quite fast. I went on up to the top and looked back over the banisters. The rats were flowing smoothly up the stairs after me.

I tip-toed across the landing, though the carpets were so thick that I need hardly have bothered. Very gently and quietly I turned the door handle of what I knew must be the Malcomsons' own bedroom. I pressed against it. Nothing happened. The door was locked.

So that was what he meant—'He can't get in *here*.'

Gently again I released the handle. Baffled? No. A locked door wasn't going to stop me. Almost immediately I remembered that I had forgotten something. Telling Socrates and Ben to keep the rats where they were I ran downstairs and very soon found the main switchboard. I turned off all the lights. Using a small pocket electric torch I came upstairs again.

I pointed to the bottom of the door with the little ring of light from my electric torch. 'Tear it,' I said. 'In you go.'

Immediately the gnawing started. I stood back and listened. I didn't have to wait long. A creak from the bed. 'Darling, are you awake?'

No reply. Whose head was under the clothes this time?

'Darling, are you awake? There's a most awfully funny noise.'

'Dig her in the ribs, man. It won't do her a bit of harm.' This of course was under my breath, but you'd have thought he had heard me.

At any rate he must have done something. For wifey awoke. 'What's the matter, dearest?'

'Listen darling. Do you not hear something?'

The scraping and gnawing went on.

'You'd think there was something trying to get through the door. Do you think Toby could have escaped?'

'If it was Toby he'd bark or something. First that car, then this. We'll get no sleep tonight.'

'No,' I murmured, just loud enough for myself to hear.

'Turn on the light, dearest, and see what on earth it is.'

Pause while Hubby tried to turn on the light. 'It won't work, darling. There must be a power cut.'

Another pause. The rats were really making a terrific noise.

'Dearest, do you not think you'd better see what it is?'

'Stop,' I whispered to the rats. There was a moment of dead silence.

The bed creaked and I heard Hubby's feet hit the floor. I waited for him to turn the key and open the door, but instead I heard his voice again. 'It seems to have stopped, darling.' He must have been standing by the edge of the bed, funking it.

'Tear it,' I whispered again to the rats, and the din started once more. If he waited another minute they'd be through under the door, and into the room whether he opened up or not. That might make things more difficult.

Suddenly I realised the door was opening. I'd never heard the key. I suppose the rats were making too much noise. Now was the critical moment. If he tried to close the door again I'd have to put my shoulder to it and make sure that he couldn't. But he didn't try. He felt rats crawling over his feet and jumped back into the room. I gave the door a push and peered in, being careful not to show myself.

Hubby gave a scream. 'It's rats, millions of them.' For a moment I saw him against the light of the window—they didn't even draw the curtains—sort of dancing on the floor. Then he jumped on to the bed.

It was wifey's turn to scream. Whether he landed on her or whether it was just the word 'Rats,' I don't know. Next moment she was standing up on the bed beside him.

I got down on my hands and knees and began to crawl through the door. 'Do something,' she screamed. Whether she saw *me* or not I don't know. I kept as close to the floor as possible and was careful not to look up. I didn't want them to see my face.

'What *can* I do?' Hubby wailed.

No dearests and darlings now. As they say, it takes very little to remove the thin veneer of civilisation.

I wriggled across the floor to the edge of the bed. It was rather a high bed for nowadays. I got half underneath it, and then, lying on my back, I began to lift rats on to the bed. I put Ben up first. He's a nasty, vicious brute, and he went straight for Hubby's toes. Hubby gave another scream—he was a good screamer that man—and did the leap of the century into the middle of the floor. He must have landed on a rat because there was a sort of squeal that I knew pretty well wasn't human. It didn't stop him. He ran half stumbling—over rats, I suppose—out of the door.

'You're not leaving me?' Wifey called.

'You bet he is,' I said to myself, 'and if *I* know Ben you won't be long after him.'

'The stairs seem clear,' Hubby called. 'You'd better run for it.' Then Ben got at *her* toes, and run she did. Talk of flying angels. The way she left that bed. You could call it vertical take-off.

Well I didn't want them to gather their wits together and start doing something sensible, like finding the lights were off, or getting sticks to defend themselves. So I turned the rats round and sent them down the stairs after dearest Hubby and darling Wifey. Still without showing myself, I came to the door, and after a moment or two out on to the landing to see what was happening.

As soon as they found the rats following them down the stairs Hubby and Wifey made a bolt for it right down to the hall. They stopped there for a moment, because they discovered they were a little ahead of the rats, which were hopping down rather slowly. 'You telephone,' Wifey ordered, 'while I find a coat. We may have to go outside.'

'Who'll I telephone?'

'Telephone the police of course—nine, nine, nine.'

By this time I was peering over the banisters. I could see him in a vague kind of way. He stumbled over something. I think he must have stubbed his toe, for he started cursing a bit—not very loud. 'Hell's gates! Where's the bloody thing got to?' But he found it and of course had to yell again for Wifey. 'I can't see the numbers. What'll I do now?'

'Feel, you fool! Do you not know yet the nine's next to nought.' No veneer left.

I heard him fumbling about with the phone for a bit and then he said, 'There's no dialling tone.'

She was back with her coat by this time. 'Oh give it me,' she told him.

So *she* tried. But of course the tape I had put on was doing its work. 'It's out of order,' she complained. 'Isn't it just like them? On a night like this too.'

I couldn't see the rats, but I thought they must be in the hall by this time. Sure enough Hubby gave a yell. 'Here they are. We'll have to run for it.' I heard the front door open and shut.

I went to a window over the porch. I saw them pick their way over the gravel to the grass. Once on the grass they began to run. They went on the verge beside the drive. Wifey was wearing the coat. Hubby had nothing on but his pyjamas. I went back to the bedroom and began to look round by the light of my electric torch. There was a dead rat in the middle of the floor. Hubby must have broken its back when he jumped out of bed. I left it there for evidence. The money was on the dressing table. I shoved it in my pocket. Also on the dressing table were two books of travellers' cheques. No use to me. I got Socrates to nibble a bit off each and dropped them on the floor.

I ran down the stairs, switched on the lights again, and untaped the telephone. I went out the front door and looked up and down. It wasn't very dark. I could see as far as the edge of the trees fairly distinctly. I felt reasonably sure there was no one about. I went round to the back and got into the car. All this time I had Socrates in my pocket. I drove round to the front door, going dead slow for the last little bit, just in case any of the rats had strayed out on to the gravel. I went into the house again and called to the rats. In five minutes they were all in the car. I looked round the hall fairly quickly to see that none had been left behind—but I didn't really care a great deal if one or two got lost. The only one that really mattered to me as an individual was Socrates, plus Ben in the sense that he's useful.

I started the car and drove slowly as far as the edge of the trees. I didn't put on the car lights. If the Malcomsons were still about I didn't want to attract their attention. They might come snooping along and take the number of the car. As soon as the car was under the trees I switched off the engine. There was a slope all the way to the gate and I hoped to get out on to the road without attracting attention. I couldn't see very well and I had to keep my foot on the brake so as not to go too fast. There was a slight danger that I might run over the Malcomsons, but I felt they should be well out along the road by this time.

I got to the road and it was still downhill. I didn't have to turn on the engine. The car rolled on gently and silently towards the city. I passed a cottage. Someone was battering at the door. 'Please let us in. Please. . . .' I heard no more—nothing but the swish of the car tyres. I began to laugh. The cottagers must be heavy sleepers. Maybe an agricultural labourer who had worked hard in the fields all day. Or maybe they were frightened to open the door. I mean there are all sorts of strange characters about nowadays. Or perhaps the cottage was empty. It wasn't a really cold night. But I thought of him in his pyjamas and her with not much more—and both with bare feet.

I suppose we free-wheeled another half-mile before I switched on the headlights and the engine. We got home without incident.

My raid on the Malcomsons is a sensation. The local evening paper
had it on the front page, with big headlines, and it's in all the
national dailies this morning. No one knows what to make of it.
Everyone is a little frightened. It's come out that there have been
previous rat-raids—the courting couple we chased from their car,
Jones's tyres, the grocer. . . . Everything is being added together
including a lot of things that have no connection with *my* rats at all.
Damage in food stores, damage to crops, babies bitten by rats in
slums. The country has suddenly become rat-conscious. The Malcomsons are both in hospital suffering from shock and exposure.
Their condition is stated not to be serious.

Jones has been interviewed on T.V. It appears the police *did* ask
him to keep quiet about his tyres. They couldn't make up their
minds if it was rats or a malicious human. It's a wonder I was
never questioned. But it wouldn't occur to Jones that I might have
a grudge against him. Little friend of all the world, I don't think.
'Now,' he says (from the T.V. screen) 'the time for secrecy is past.
Everyone must get together and put an end to this scandal.'

The papers are still going on about the rats. It is being suggested
that the rat population far outnumbers the human population.
At any moment the rats of the world may arise and murder the
humans while the humans lie asleep in their beds. 'These vermin
must be eradicated. They are costing a hungry world millions of
lives every year.' One paper calls for a World Rat Year.

Mrs. Malcomson has been interviewed on her release from hospital. They are to stay with friends for a few days, before deciding
whether to continue with their holiday or not. There is a photograph of her clasping Toby. Toby is licking her face. But that's not
the point. She insists that there was one huge rat as big as a man,
which crawled slowly across the floor from the door to the bed.
Obviously the interviewers didn't know what to make of this.
There's a headline, 'Rat as big as man,' in one paper, and another
has, 'Rat Monster.' It goes on, 'Asked what the Rat monster looked
like, Mrs. Malcomson said it was "Quite obscene".' This of course
is me. What does she mean, 'Obscene?' Incidentally Hubby didn't
see any 'Rat Monster.' The way it's put in the interview makes it

plain that he doesn't think his wife did either, though he's polite enough not actually to say so.

Only today did I realise the significance of the appearance of Toby in the photograph with Mrs. Malcomson. As usual the information came from Jones via the Book-keeper. Jones is enjoying a kind of double fame at present. First of all he knows the Malcomsons. That's quite something these days. And as the Malcomsons are so well off it gives you a standing socially as well as conversationally—and of course he's a rat victim himself. That ensures immediate attention. He says if he'd known what was happening to his tyres he'd have gone out and laid about him with a stick. 'They're quite easy to deal with if you don't lose your head. A cut with the stick, and you snap the backbone. Just like that.'

'But are you not afraid of them going for your throat, Mr. Jones? They say they can tear your throat out with their teeth and you're dead in a matter of seconds.' This from the girl, looking at Jones as if he was her hero. It'd sicken you. Jones and the Book-keeper standing talking in the middle of the Cash Office. The girl gazing up adoringly and openly eaves-dropping.

'I don't think any rat would go for *my* throat,' declared the brave and gallant Jones. 'It would have short thrift if it did.'

It appears that the dog Toby was booked for the gas chamber while sweet Wifey and Hubby were hitting the high spots in London. They were fond of poor Toby and he wasn't particularly old. But they couldn't afford to pay for him in boarding kennels while they were away. The R.S.P.C.A. was going to keep him for a week free. Then, if nobody wanted him, put him down painlessly. The Malcomsons would have got a new puppy after they came back and had time to settle down. Far more fun than placid old Toby.

Now remorse has struck. Toby was uneasy the night before the raid. Perhaps even then the rats were prowling and about to strike. Brave dog Toby rushed out barking without a thought for his own safety and drove them off. So brave dog Toby, protector of dear Master and Mistress, who really love him deeply, is to be preserved to an honoured old age. This of course didn't appear in the papers, but all the Malcomsons' friends, who it seems are in the habit of dealing with their own dogs in the same way, have been talking about it. So *I* saved Toby's life.

The idea of a rat monster has been taken up seriously by two of the Sunday papers. 'What *did* Mrs. Malcomson see?' The other, more effectively, I thought, 'What Mrs. Malcomson saw.' Fair makes your flesh creep, don't it! What she saw, it appears, was a monster half-human half-rat. 'Scientists have long been aware that legendary creatures, such as the mysterious "Monster of Glamis", really do exist. Their occurrence fortunately is rare, but when they occur they present a fearful menace to humanity. In the present instance it would seem that such a creature is loose in our midst, a monster rat-man. . . .'

There was a whole lot more, all pseudo-scientific in a very crude sort of way. I don't know how much faith anyone puts in it. Probably the less educated swallow it whole, while the highbrows reject it absolutely. No matter. But everyone has started to talk of 'Ratman', and whether they really believe in Ratman or not, everyone's on the look-out for him.

The girl certainly is. 'What do *you* think of Ratman?' she asked me.

I determined to be bold. The way to throw them off the trail is certainly not to pretend *I* don't believe in Ratman. 'I think he's hiding somewhere.'

'D'you reely?'

'Yes. I expect he's lying up, waiting to strike again.'

Because of all the excitement I won't bring Socrates and Ben into the office any more just at present. Someone might notice their droppings and then there'd be a general hunt. I miss Socrates when I'm working late—and that's nearly every night, except Friday.

When I went up to bed last night with Socrates I found Ben curled up in the middle of the eiderdown, sound asleep. At first I didn't know what to do. Ben is a very different rat from Socrates. I don't know why, but I have always felt slightly afraid of him. Wakened suddenly he might turn and snap. I've never been bitten by one of the rats yet and I don't want to be.

After watching Ben for a moment or two I put Socrates down on the pillow and gave the eiderdown a sharp tug. Ben awoke, sprang up, and glared at me most angrily. At first I was frightened. Ben looked as if he meant to fight it out. But I knew I mustn't be frightened. If I started letting myself be frightened of the rats what on earth would be the end of it? So I said sternly, 'Ben, you know very well you're not allowed here,' and picked him up as I was speaking. He did snap at me, but he took good care not to bite. I gave him a little tap on the head with my forefinger and repeated, 'Bad Ben,' once or twice. Then I carried him downstairs and put him into the cellar with the others.

I went to bed, with Socrates beside me as usual, and fell asleep almost immediately. But when I awoke this morning Ben was back on the bed, under the eiderdown this time, on the opposite side of me to Socrates.

I lay quiet for a little, thinking what to do. Apart from Socrates I don't want to give the rats the run of the house. Particularly I don't want them in my bedroom, and more particularly still I don't want them all crawling over the bed. 'I'll teach you,' I thought suddenly, and I gave a great big kick under the clothes just where Ben was lying. Ben shot out towards the middle of the floor landing there with a fair bang. 'That'll larn you to do what you're told,' I shouted at him.

Next moment I was sorry. I was afraid that the fall might have done him an injury, but it didn't seem to have. He looked stunned for a moment or two, but perhaps it was because he hadn't quite wakened up. Then he gave me a look that was anything but cowed—in fact it was diabolical—and went slowly off behind the dressing table.

I hadn't time to do anything about him then. I had to hurry to get into work, but when I came home this evening he was back with the other rats in the cellar. It was obvious how he had got both out and in. There was a hole gnawed in the bottom of the cellar-door. I spent the evening patching it up. Then I covered the whole bottom of the door with tin—two old biscuit-tins which I cut up for the purpose and fixed on with tacks. We'll see how he likes tin and tacks to sharpen his teeth on.

This morning I again found Ben on the bed. He wasn't asleep. He was watching me. For a while we both remained quite still, our eyes fixed on each other. A sudden kick would be no good this time. The slightest movement on my part would be met by a counter move. I wondered what he would do if I drew up my left leg so as to get it into position to give him a hefty kick like yesterday morning's. Would he jump quickly over to my right side where Socrates was still sound asleep, or would he go at my throat which was uncovered, and try to kill me? I didn't think he could succeed. I would get my hand up pretty quickly. Still it was a nasty thought. Ben looked very fierce. His teeth were slightly bared and his hair was standing on end. Perhaps the nips he had had at the Malcomsons' toes had given him a taste for human blood. If Ben did attack would Socrates help me? I was sure at any rate that he wouldn't join in against me.

Keeping my eyes fixed on Ben I edged slightly over towards Socrates. Socrates woke up, uncurled and stretched himself. He licked his hands and began to wash his face. Ben dug his claws into the quilt and gripped it tightly. I realised at once that he had no intention of attacking me, only of holding on like grim death. Well I had no intention of projecting him into the middle of the floor a second time. I had no wish to hurt him.

I slipped out of bed at the right-hand side disturbing Socrates as little as possible. Socrates continued the regular routine of his grooming. I had no time to deal with Ben just then. It's always a rush getting out of the house in the morning. I suppose I should train myself to wake up earlier. Ben will have to be taught who's master, but it will have to wait till tomorrow morning. Now I know he doesn't mean to attack me I know exactly what to do. I am going to take up Father's old walking-stick when I go to bed tonight. I shall leave it across the end of the bed behind my pillow, where I can reach it in the morning almost without moving. Ben's in for a nasty surprise. Not that I shall do him any harm, just teach him a lesson.

But I don't know how he got out. The tin's still there on the bottom of the door.

The walking stick was effective. I set myself to wake up much earlier than usual and was successful. There was Ben lying on the quilt at my left side. He was awake too. I pulled myself up sharply in the bed and grabbed the stick. Ben dug his claws in, prepared to hold on. I don't think he had any idea what I was going to do. I got into a half-kneeling position and gave him a first quite gentle prod with the stick. Ben snapped at it. I prodded him again a little harder—and then harder, and harder. . . . He tried to get hold of the stick in his mouth, but he couldn't. He kept on snapping. He tried to dodge round the point of the stick—there was a ferrule on it—but I kept making quick, whippy movements with my wrist so that he couldn't get past. Inexorably I forced him back towards the end of the bed, careful all the time to do him no real damage. I could see he was furious. Given half a chance he would have counter-attacked with teeth and claws. But I gave him no chance and all of a sudden he realised he couldn't win. He turned and ran down a piece of hanging blanket, jumping the last six or nine inches to the floor. Then he went under the bed.

Now what to do? If I settled down and went to sleep he'd be up again in a moment. I'd have to get him right out of the room, teach him that this was no place for *him*. If I got up in the ordinary way I felt quite convinced that as soon as my toes came dangling down the side of the bed Ben would have a go at them, nipping them as he'd done with Malcomson. Incidentally my bed's pretty high, higher even than the Malcomsons', an iron bed with brass knobs at the corners so that there's normally quite a bit of dangling time before my feet reach the floor. Incidentally again, I'm sure it's much easier to make than a modern bed, because you don't have to bend down so far.

I decided to leap suddenly into the middle of the floor. Grasping the stick firmly in my right hand I leaped (leapt?). I turned round quickly and crouched down, facing the bed. At the side nearest to me the bedclothes had slipped right down to the floor so that I couldn't see underneath. Socrates, who had slept all through my duel with Ben, had at last woken up. He came to the edge of the bed and peered down at me, looking rather puzzled. I advanced to the bed, swishing the stick backwards and forwards, or rather sideways and sideways, along the floor, watching every minute for Ben to jump out from under the bed and renew the battle. Ben didn't show himself. I swished the stick right along under the edge of the clothes. I felt nothing. I swished again, a little further in. Again nothing. I advanced a little more, thrust the whole length of the stick under the bed, and waggled it furiously. Sound of stick against china. I caught the hanging blankets and sheet with the point of the stick and flicked them one by one on to the top of the bed. This a little inconvenienced Socrates, who found himself getting covered in bedclothes and had to retreat to my pillow where his view of the proceedings was not nearly so good. I peered under the bed. There was no one there—nothing in fact but Edgar Allan, which I hardly ever use because of the nuisance of emptying it. Well he might be in there. It's a nice flowery one with a handle. I reversed the stick, attached the crook to Edgar's handle and pulled. No. Ben wasn't there. He must have scurried out the opposite side during the time it was hidden from me by the bedclothes.

I spent nearly an hour searching the room for Ben. I didn't find him. When at last I got back to bed it was within half an hour of getting-up time and I didn't get any more sleep. As I usually do, unless I'm very late, I made my bed before going down for breakfast. I left the stick along the top behind the pillow as before, but perhaps tomorrow morning I shan't need it.

Last night I was late getting to bed. I was home late after working in the office till nearly ten, and I suppose being tired slowed me down. I took longer than usual dealing with the rats in the cellar. Also in writing my notes. After that I fell asleep in my chair. Socrates woke me up by scratching my hand with his paw—very gently at first so that I dreamed that there was a fly walking over my hand and then that I had been bitten by a clegg. I thought that there would be no harm in taking him into the office again—and Ben too of course to keep him company. All the talk about rats seems to have died away and the plan for a great rat-purge put forward by one of the papers has been forgotten.

I went upstairs. I hadn't been in my bedroom since the morning and the first thing I did was to look for Father's stick behind the pillow. In a way it was there, and in a way it wasn't. It had been divided into little bits each not more than one inch long. There were smaller bits all over the place. I showed it to Socrates and you could almost see him shaking his head in disapproval. 'That young rat will come to a bad end,' he was saying to himself. I burst out laughing. You had to hand it to Ben. He was unbeatable. Or thought he was.

Then I chuckled quietly to myself. Thought he had me beat, did he? Well he'd another think coming. I'd show him.

I nipped downstairs and got the poker from the sitting room. It's not used any more, because I've no time to light coal fires. So it was quite clean. I put it behind the pillow, where the stick had been. I undressed very quickly, got into bed and turned out the light. I intended to stay awake for a little, though not very long, because I was tired and meant to get my sleep. But I had an idea that before very long Friend Ben would turn up for a nice sleep on the eiderdown. I had a pretty shrewd idea that he got into my room through a hole in the floor under the dressing table. It was no good covering it with tin. He'd just make another hole some-where else—and I couldn't cover the whole floor with tin.

At first I felt quite excited, but soon I began to get sleepy. I was thinking, 'It'll do just as well in the morning,' and practically dozing off when I heard a scuffly sort of noise from the direction of the dressing table. 'Here you come my boy,' I thought, 'and you're in for a big surprise.'

I heard his feet patter across the floor. No pause to reconnoitre. He was quite sure I was sound asleep by this time. Not that recon-noitring would have done him any good. I was pretending to be asleep. He jumped straight on to the bed. Not on to the top. Just high enough to get his claws in, and I felt the slight drag on the bedclothes as he scrambled up the rest of the way. Quite a jump all the same. Then he found the same place on top of the eiderdown and spent quite a time going round and round making a kind of nest for himself. When everything was arranged to his satisfaction he settled down for his night's sleep. 'Well,' I thought. 'Getting a bit careless, aren't you? Don't care if you wake me up or not.'

I waited till I thought he'd just about be into his beauty sleep. Then I sat up quickly, turned on the bedside light and waved the poker over my head.

You should have seen the expression on his face. It was ludi-crous. He didn't wait to argue. One look was enough. He didn't

want the poker in his ribs. Dive, and he was on the floor. He
scuttled across it and under the dressing table. 'And you needn't
come back,' I called after him. 'You won't eat through the poker in
a hurry.'

That was last night. Tonight—I don't quite know why. I suppose
just to make sure he hadn't gnawed through the poker—I went
straight up to my bedroom as soon as I got in. The poker wasn't
there. What's more, there wasn't a single poker in the whole house.

There were tongs of course, brass curtain-rods, shovels. . . . But
I decided to admit defeat. Whatever I choose as a weapon to take
to bed with me will be spirited away during the day. An occasion
may arise when I shall need a curtain-rail. There's no sense showing Ben how a curtain-rail could be used.

In any case I think I shall take both Ben and Socrates into the
office tomorrow. All the fuss about rats seems to have died down. I
don't see why they shouldn't be perfectly safe in the Bookroom. In
fact they'd have been safe there all along. I've never seen anyone go
in except myself—and I don't think anyone has seen me. It'll keep
Ben out of mischief—and stop him from leading the other rats
into mischief. Because I'm quite sure he couldn't have purloined
the poker all by himself. Even as a combined effort it was a considerable feat.

For the last month I have been taking Socrates and Ben into the
office with me every day except Fridays. I go in a little early in the
morning and pop them into the Bookroom before anyone arrives.
At night, when everyone else has gone, I bring them into the Cash
Office with me and let them run about there while I work.

But on Fridays Jones himself works late. So I might have difficulty getting them out of the Bookroom again without being seen.
I don't know what Jones *does* every Friday night, but he insists on
having the whole place to himself. All the rest of us have to leave
promptly at half-past five. I'm sure he's up to some fiddle or other.
I wish I could find out what.

I don't understand the relative positions of Ben and Socrates.
I've always supposed that Ben was the son of Socrates. But they

might be brothers. My main reason for thinking them father and son is that I haven't seen old Ma Rat since the very beginning—long before Ben appeared—and I've assumed she must be dead. I think Ben is cleverer than Socrates. Certainly he is more cunning, more independent. He and Socrates appear perfectly friendly, but I wonder if Ben has taken over as Boss. I don't mean Boss over Socrates himself, but Boss over the other rats—King Rat you might say. If this is so I think it must be since our last escapade. I wonder if it had anything to do with the fact that we had one rat killed. Could they possibly *mind* about that?

Today the girl came into the Cash Office and said she'd heard a scuffling noise from the Bookroom when she was in the Ladies next door. Were there mice in there? I said it had always been full of mice, but that there was sheet iron nailed on to the partition between it and the Ladies' so that no mice could get in. This satisfied her. Of course there's no sheet iron, and I don't know if there have ever been any mice either. But I think it was rather clever of me to dream all that up on the spur of the moment. It'll stop her making a complaint to Jones or the Book-keeper, and it will probably prevent *her*, or any of the other girls even venturing into the Bookroom. Of course she couldn't get in without the key. But she's pretty nosey and might easily have found some excuse to get the place opened up.

Saying she's nosey doesn't mean I don't find her attractive. I do. In fact if I were differently situated, that is to say if I had sufficient money and there were no rats, I would probably ask her to marry me. I only realised this today just after I had told her the tale about the mice. Of course what she really heard was Ben, or Socrates, or both.

I said to her, 'Oh there's a little mouse on the floor now!' She immediately gave a shriek and jumped on to a chair. Perhaps I thought that would happen. Perhaps I wanted it to happen. At any rate she looked very pretty up there, and appealing. She has shapely legs, just a shade on the thin side, I suppose, by Beauty Queen standards but there's something about her knees. . . . Anyhow I had a good stare. Then I told her I was only joking. She gave me a sort of arch look and stepped down very daintily. I'm quite sure she didn't mind a bit. Any chance to show themselves off. That's what girls like. In fact I can't see how modern girls need to worry about mice. It might have been different when they were afraid of mice running up inside their skirts, but it would be a very athletic mouse who could ever reach a modern skirt, a pole-jumping mouse perhaps, if you can imagine such a thing—and I can quite easily.

The girl by the way is still very interested in me. I'd just have to say the word and she'd come for a drive in the car like a shot, tea or no tea.

I can hardly bear to write down what's happened. But I will. It was the girl's fault. Her and Jones. Jones did it.

I didn't hear any shriek, not from the girl I mean, but I'm sure there was one. The first I noticed was a bit of commotion in the passage. Nothing much. One or two people hurrying and talking, and one of them was the girl. I know her voice. I didn't pay any attention. I went on with my work.

Next I heard Jones proceeding down the passage. I know his step, always a little more dignified. This was enough for the Book-keeper. If Jones was going he was going too. Out he went. I was feeling rather contemptuous and stand-offish, determined not to follow the crowd, ready to say in a languid voice when they got back, 'Well, and what was all that fuss about?' All the same I wondered very much what was up and was having quite a fight with my own curiosity.

Then suddenly it occurred to me, 'Has someone gone into the Bookroom and found Socrates?' Till this moment the two rats hadn't entered my thoughts. I had grown so accustomed to leaving them in the Bookroom every day, without anything happening. And I felt sure no one but myself had been in the Bookroom for years.

I jumped up and rushed down to the back. There they all were, Jones, the Book-keeper, the whole staff. The door of the Ladies was open—not the actual W.C. door, but the place where they wash their hands and make tea, and I suppose, actually do powder their noses. Inside were Jones and the girl, both looking up. 'Here,' Jones said. 'Someone get me a long stick or a rod or something. I'll soon fix it.'

At first I couldn't see anything, but I'd awful forebodings. I edged a little closer, pushing past the Book-keeper, who seemed to be drawing back. High up on top of the wall behind the basin in a little recess between two rafters was Socrates. He was quite still and you'd wonder the girl had noticed him. Of course that's the sort of her. Notices everything.

To anyone but me Socrates would probably have seemed quite unruffled. But his hair was all standing on end and I knew he was very frightened. I guessed at once what had happened. Rafters run across under the roof of the Ladies and into the wall which divides it from the Bookroom. Both are one-storey additions to the main building which jut out into the yard behind the offices. The wall is two bricks thick, but for some reason there is no top row of bricks on the Ladies side. This makes a row of little recesses and one of them goes right through to the Bookroom. In fact there's one brick missing from the top row on the Bookroom side as well. All this of course I've discovered since. Socrates must have come through the hole, possibly looking for water. I'd never thought of leaving them water. On the wall above the basins was a big old mirror about four feet broad, with a thick black wooden frame, three to four inches deep. After coming through the tunnel from the Bookroom Socrates must have jumped down on to the top of this, run along it, and by a series of small leaps got down to the basin for his drink. On the way back—perhaps he had been flustered by the girl coming in and turning on the light—he had missed the tunnel and gone into the recess next to it, a dead end. All he had to do now to escape was to come out, jump down again on to the top of the mirror, run along five or six inches, hop up into the next recess and run through to the safety of the Bookroom. Well it would be safe for the time being. They'd have a job finding him in there among hundreds of old books, receipt files, bags full of old letters. . . .

I didn't know what to do. I could have spoken to Socrates, calmed him, told him to come out quickly before it was too late and run along the top of the mirror to the next recess. For I knew that the office junior had gone off to look for the rod or stick that Jones had demanded. I could even have climbed up on to the top of the basins and coaxed Socrates out. I could have pretended I was trying to catch him and then pretended to be angry when he

wriggled out of my hands and escaped through the tunnel. I didn't
think of that. Not till afterwards, when it was too late. But I did
think of speaking to him. I didn't dare. Everyone at once, as soon
as they saw that Socrates understood my instructions and obeyed
them, would have known that there really was a Ratman, that *I*
was Ratman. So I stood in an agony of dither and fear, and said
nothing.

The boy came back with a metal rod, a thin tube of some kind,
about six feet long. 'The very thing!' Jones exclaimed.

He took the rod and made a sort of exploratory poke, not very
hard, into the recess. And then I knew that he had seen me—I
mean that Socrates had seen me. He threw me a sort of look as if
to say, 'Aren't you going to stop him?' And of course I could have
stopped him. I'm bigger than Jones—and a good deal younger.

But I did nothing. I didn't even say, 'Stop!' I was afraid. I was a
coward.

The next poke, though still only experimental, was a little harder.
Socrates drew back into the recess and made himself smaller.
You'd hardly have known he was there. At the third poke Socrates
screamed.

The scream seemed to excite Jones. 'I've got him now,' he said.
'He doesn't like *that*. I'll give him a bit more of the same medi-
cine.' And he began to prod at Socrates quite furiously.

At last Socrates tried to come out, first at one side of the little
recess, and then at the other. But Jones by a sort of brilliant exhi-
bition of swordsmanship drove him back. And every time Jones
prodded Socrates screamed. When he drew back after the second
attempt to get out the screaming became continuous.

'Oh do stop, please Mr. Jones,' the girl exclaimed suddenly.

Jones was astonished. 'Why do you want me to stop?' he asked.

'Just it's too horrible. It's cruel.'

'It's not cruel at all,' Jones replied. 'Rats are vermin. Got to be
exterminated.' He went on prodding.

The next time I saw the end of the rod it was covered in blood.
But Socrates wasn't dead. He was still screaming. I drew back. I
couldn't bear to watch any more, but I couldn't go away. I felt that
even if I didn't dare to do anything it would be wrong to go away.
I had to see Socrates dead. He took a long time to die.

The screaming stopped. 'Has he kicked it?' the boy asked—the boy who'd brought the rod. You could see he was thoroughly enjoying it all, grinning all over his face.

'Not a bit of him,' Jones answered. 'There's one of his legs still moving. But I'll soon finish him off now.'

There was no more screaming, just the prodding, and soon that stopped. Jones was satisfied that Socrates was dead.

'How are you going to get him out?' the boy asked.

'Oh I'll get him out all right.' He thrust the bloody rod once more into the recess and pushed hard. Then he drew it out again and impaled on the end of it was a mess of blood and fur and guts. For a moment Jones forgot his dignity and brandished it at the girls. 'How do you like that?'

They all shrieked and drew back, but they weren't really horrified. Some of them even smiled a little.

'You've made an awful mess of our cloakroom,' one of the typists said. 'Who's going to clean it up?'

'You are,' Jones said. 'If you don't know how to use a mop it's about time you learnt.'

They all seemed in doubt for a moment, but the girl went off and got a mop from the cupboard under the stairs—and I saw one of the typists with a bucket. The rest of us went back to our work.

I didn't work late tonight. To tell the truth I could hardly work at all. But I had to wait till all the others had gone before I could fetch Ben out of the Bookroom. I felt almost like leaving him behind. I didn't want to have anything to do with him, anything to do with anything that had to do with what had happened. But of course I couldn't leave him.

And when I went to the Bookroom I was suddenly sorry for him. Poor Ben was terrified. No wonder. He was even terrified of me. If he hadn't seen everything he had heard everything—and after all who had prodded *him* with a stick and a poker in the bedroom at home? Who had stood by and done nothing while Socrates was prodded to death? Who had brought them both into this dangerous place?

So Ben looked at me fearfully. Obviously he wanted, must want, to go home, away from this gruesome place. But could he trust me to take him, or would I deliver him up to be done to death as I had let Socrates be done to death? Perhaps I would even kill him myself.

It took half-an-hour of coaxing to get him into the bag, and then of course I took him straight home. I've spent all evening with him trying to soothe him. I never really liked him before, but now Socrates has gone I feel a new affection for him. I see that he may even come to take the place of Socrates with me.

Last night after I went to bed I lay awake wondering if Ben would come and join me. It would show whether he trusted me or not. For a long time I was alone. Then I heard a slight noise and knew Ben was under the dressing table. I lay and waited. It crossed my mind that if he didn't trust me Ben might gather an army of rats there, wait till I was asleep, come out and tear my throat. I went on listening. But there was no sound of other rats.

At last I heard Ben crossing the floor. Though I had left the blanket hanging down for him specially, it was a long time before I felt the slight tug as he jumped and caught it and began to climb up. But he came in the end. I felt him curl up and settle himself beside me. I put out my hand and stroked the fur along his backbone with one finger, the way I had been accustomed to do with Socrates.

I hate Jones.

I hate Jones. I hate him very much.

I hate Jones. He has killed the only creature in the world I ever really loved.

I hate Jones. Somehow, some day I am going to kill him.

Today the girl and I discussed Jones. We were alone together in the Cash Office in the lunch-hour. 'Do you like him?' I asked bluntly.

'I wouldn't like to be married to him,' she answered surprisingly. At least I was surprised at first. I was surprised she should say such a thing to me at all. I thought this was the sort of thing girls said to other girls. She had obviously considered what Jones would be like as a husband—in spite of the fact that she knew there was a

Mrs. Jones already. I took it therefore she meant exactly the opposite to what she had said. In fact she wished she could be married
to Jones, but as she knew she couldn't she was saying she wouldn't
like to be.

I tried to think what a female confidante would have said in
the circumstances and quickly hit upon what I think was the right
reply. 'Of course he's too old for you.'

She sighed. 'He's such a brute.'

'He's a sadist,' I retorted, and then, as that didn't seem to mean
anything to her, 'He delights in being cruel.'

'He's very masculine,' she said. 'I think men *are* cruel.'

'Not any more cruel than women. He's debased, perverted. . . .
Did you see the way . . . ?' And then I stopped. I couldn't go on. I
almost burst into tears. Shame. Grief. I don't know which was the
strongest.

'You mean killing the rat the other day?'

I nodded.

'Yes. That was brutal—but that's what I mean.'

'You tried to stop him,' I reminded her.

'I know—and I couldn't. He didn't understand. He wasn't being
sadistic. He was just the dominant male, the fighting male smash-
ing his foe. If it had been another man it would have been just the
same.'

I gave a sarcastic sort of laugh. 'Another man would have stood
up to him. Anyone can be a hero fighting something as small as, as
small as . . .'

'As small as that rat. I don't know. A lot of people are afraid of
rats, specially since this scare. Jones didn't hesitate a moment. I
think he's brave, you know. I didn't notice that any of the other
men were very anxious to do anything for us. And someone had to
do something. We couldn't leave the rat there, in the Ladies. Someone had to kill it.'

'Oh yes of course.' For a moment it had been on the tip of my
tongue to say, 'Why?' But that might have given me away. I added,
'All the same it wasn't necessary to kill it so brutally.'

'I don't think most men would have thought him brutal,' she
answered. 'You're more sensitive than most men. He was just being
manly.'

To be called sensitive is not really a compliment. I'm sure the girl finds Jones's brutality attractive. It gives her a thrill. She imagines herself clasped in the arms of the brutal Jones. . . .

Well I'm going to be just as brutal as the heroic Jones one of these days. We'll see how he likes a bit of brutality when he's on the receiving end. He won't like it at all, but he'll never get a chance to tell anyone.

I'm going to be short of money again, not immediately, but in four to six months. I see it coming. The car uses up an awful lot of money, but I need it. I couldn't use the rats without it. And the rats themselves take money. I'll have to keep doing things—to get money I mean. It's no good waiting till I'm desperate. I'll have to keep the supply going, make sure I've always something in hand. So I'm thinking out something else to do. It really should be quite easy. The thing is to make sure I'm not traced and caught. I'm making plans for Jones too.

Today (Sunday) I was looking for fuse-wire. I remembered that Father used to keep some in a sort of odds-and-ends box he had. I couldn't think where it had got to and then I decided to have a look to see if it was in some of the old trunks in the boxroom. I got it in the end, but when I was looking for it I came across a rather odd thing. I didn't know what it was at first. It's a false head, like those false faces children wear, only bigger and more elaborate.

I slipped it on. There are little eyeholes to look out by. I went to a looking-glass and looked at myself. I gazed for quite a long time before I realised what the head was meant to be. It is grotesque, and makes me seem taller than I really am. There are painted eyes (not the holes I look out of, which are quite cleverly concealed). In the centre of these eyes is glass which glitters and gives quite a ghastly effect. The snout is rather sharp and points upwards. There are whiskers, each whisker stuck on separately, and ears made of real fur. At last I recognised what it is meant to represent—the head of a rat. In fact apart from the size, which is many times too big, it's most realistic. If you looked at it through the wrong end of a telescope you'd think it really *was* a rat's head. If it hadn't been for the size I should have recognised it immediately.

What puzzles me is why it should have been there at all. I suppose it was got for some fancy-dress party long ago. But I can't remember any fancy-dress party. Or could it have been amateur theatricals. I seem to remember vaguely hearing about an amateur dramatic society in connection with the church—before I was born probably. I've got an idea Father and Mother had something to do with it. Perhaps they did *The Wind in the Willows*, which would have seemed quite modern in those days.

I brought the rat-head down and put it on a chair in my bedroom. A vague idea was beginning to take shape in my brain. There was always the danger that on one of my raids I might be seen and recognised. Why not a disguise? And what better disguise than this? It would fit in with the Ratman legend, which was still lingering on. It would make things harder for the police. Should they believe in the Ratman theory, or reject it? What evidence could they believe? The more fantastic I could make things the more foxed they would be.

Of course if I ever come under suspicion and the house is searched the rat-head is going to make pretty damning evidence against me—if I've used it that is. But then the house is full of damning evidence. What would they make of the cellar?

It can't make things any worse to use it, and it might help a lot.

After Socrates was killed, I thought for a bit that Ben might partly take his place. I knew I couldn't immediately have the same feeling for him as I had for Socrates, but I felt affectionate towards him and hoped that he might begin to feel affectionate towards me.

So far there has been no sign of anything of the sort. He doesn't mind being stroked, and of course he continues to sleep on my bed as a sort of right. Old Socrates wouldn't have minded if *all* the rats shared my bed with him, but I'm sure Ben won't tolerate any sharing. My bed is his throne, or royal palace, I don't quite know which. All *I* am is the central heating. It's funny to think that, if he wanted, he could quite easily turn me out of my own bed. If it came to that he could turn me out of the house, or even kill me. . . .

I sometimes wonder what he thinks. He thinks a lot. I know that. Sometimes I find him looking at me with one of those little brown eyes. He nearly always does look at me sideways, one eye at a time. I feel like a top Russian under Stalin. It can't have been very nice to find suddenly that Stalin was looking at you—and wonder what he was thinking.

Perhaps Ben blames me for the death of Socrates. I could have saved Socrates. Ben maybe thinks I didn't want to, that I wanted them both killed. Or else that I wanted *him* killed—and Socrates got killed instead by accident. The way Jones did it was so like the way I prodded Ben when I was chasing him off the bed. Of course I wouldn't have gone on, really to injure him. But how does Ben know that? As he sees it he was lucky enough or clever enough to escape. Socrates couldn't. . . .

All I really know is that Ben doesn't trust me—and I don't trust him.

One of these days I'll have to do another raid. The amount of food the rats get through is perfectly appalling. They keep multiplying. I've no idea any more how many I'm feeding. Of course I'll need the rats for the raid, and I can't work the rats without Ben. Will he co-operate? How on earth can I make him understand what the raid is for? He understands food all right. If I went out raiding every night and brought the car back filled with food, he'd know what I was doing. But how can I explain to him that money is the equivalent of food, that once I have money I can get all the food we need?

I don't even know if he'll come out with me at all. I certainly don't think he'd come if he thought I was taking him to the office. Not that I'd want to take him there. There's no comfort in having Ben about. When I'm working late I'm quite glad he's not there. It's bad enough going home at night to those nasty little eyes, that long thoughtful expression.

Today I was on the jury—criminal case. Fancy me on the jury. It's because the house is now in my name. Mother got exemption on account of age or something.

I found the experience most interesting—and instructive. I listened very carefully to the police evidence. It taught me a lot about their methods, which may be useful. The chap in the dock was a mug. We found him guilty in about two minutes, no one disagreeing. The foreman said we'd better not go back too quick or the judge might think we hadn't considered the case properly. So we all chatted for a bit and then they brought us in lunch. It was quite a good lunch—soup, boiled mutton, mashed potatoes and peas. There was rice-pudding too, but I didn't have any because it had raisins in it, which I don't like. Apart from that it was the best lunch I've had since Mother died.

After lunch we went back and the foreman announced our verdict. The chap was sent to gaol for a year with suitable labour. He was a bit weakly looking. I'd have given him life. He ought never to be let out. He's not fit to look after himself, a disgrace to the criminal classes. However chaps like him help to keep the police busy and I suppose the rest of us ought to be grateful.

Acting on information received, as a policeman would say—actually it was a remark the girl made in the office—I proceeded last night (Saturday) to one of the poorer districts of 'This great city of ours' (Jones), and studied the shopping habits of the populace. The shops were doing an enormous business. The money was pouring in. I was interested to know what happened to it all after the shops closed. In some of the shops, of course, I couldn't see where it went—presumably into safes on the premises—which would be outside my line of business. A lot, I feel pretty sure, went away in private cars with the owners of the businesses—*they* might interest me on another occasion. Suppose they take the money home and keep it about the house over the week-end.

In one shop—quite a big shop too—a single light remained burning after all the others had gone out, and the staff had gone home. 'That,' I said to myself, 'is the old boy himself, in his office, counting his ill-gotten gains—probably a hundred per cent off everything and nineteen per cent per annum after that in hire purchase.'

Eventually the light went off and sure enough, from a side door, came a stooped old man. He was carrying a leather bag, which looked much too heavy for him. He shuffled along some side streets between warehouses, and came out eventually to a much brighter street. He crossed this and stopped almost immediately at a bank. He opened his bag and seemed to shove a lot of envelopes or packets through a sort of post-box in the wall. I waited till he had gone and went over to have a look. It was one of these night-safes. 'That's my man,' I said to myself, and went home to bed.

Maybe I have been silly about Ben. Maybe he has no nasty thoughts. Maybe he'd even come into the office with me again if I wanted. At any rate he came out in the car with me tonight quite willingly. Incidentally the car simply eats money, eats it and drinks it, smokes it and breathes it.

What we did tonight was another reconnaissance, partly too a rehearsal. I wanted to familiarise Ben with the terrain as the Major might say.

I parked the car in the street between the warehouses, facing the same way as the old man would be facing on his way to the bank, but on the opposite side of the road. I got out and paced the distances from each corner. I put Ben down on the pavement at the corner nearest the bank, and keeping a sharp eye out for dogs and cats got him to run back towards the car. I timed him and then timed myself walking slowly from the opposite end of the street to the same place. After that I moved the car forward a little and did it all over again. I tried to walk with a shuffling step which would be exactly the same speed as the old man from the shop.

At last I got into the car and waited. I had a long wait. Shortly after midnight the old man appeared again from the side-door of his shop. In all the time I had been there not another soul had entered that street. This suits me very well. I timed the old man from the moment he put out the light in his office till the moment he opened the door on to the street—one minute five seconds. He must do a lot of fumbling about in the dark. And from the moment he closed his own door, till he was level with the car. He walked faster than I had thought. He looked frightened too, as if very conscious of the danger he was in, carrying so much money along a dark street late at night. People go on doing these things till they do them once too often. Strangely enough he didn't seem to notice the car, parked there with its lights out. It was someone coming up from behind he was afraid of. When he had gone I drove the car forward seven yards. I made a big chalk mark on the wall level with the front wheel, but just in case it should get rubbed out during the next week I memorised the position carefully.

Home to a late supper for both of us. I write up these notes. I'm going to use the rat's head as a disguise. The first time, but not I fancy the last. We shared the bread-and-milk. There's no doubt about it, Ben is becoming more friendly.

I've been doing a bit of drill, rehearsing for Saturday night, and perhaps for future occasions as well. I can get all the rats out of the car in between twenty-five and twenty-eight seconds. It takes forty to forty-five to get them back in again.

Business isn't too bad, is it Jones? Everything's going along very nicely, isn't it Jones? No more trouble with rats at the tyres. That was a man's job you did in the office, Jones—killing the rat in the Ladies. All the girls admire you for that. There's something about a *real man* that gives them a thrill. But don't think that the rats have forgotten you, Jones. Vengeance is on the way.

Actually Jones doesn't think anything about it. That rats might have feelings would hardly occur to him. He has gone through life without being aware that people have feelings, certainly without caring whether they have them or not. So why bother about rats? Well! 'Don't care will be made to care' and before he's very much older. I haven't fixed the date yet, but I've fixed the day. It will be a Friday, in the evening. I'll find out too what he gets up to when he's all by himself in the office.

Saturday again. 11.30 p.m. All rats into the car, Ben in front with me. We drove through the City. Still a good many people about, some of them drunk. Fish and chip shops open. We reached the street of the dark warehouses. My chalk mark was still on the wall. I found it quite easily, but I didn't park there. I parked further on, almost at the corner, on the wrong side of the road. I kept my sidelights on. I hoped that nothing would come round the corner quickly and run into me.

I found that being on the same side of the street as the shop, and rather far away, I couldn't see for certain if the light in the office was on or off. I got out of the car. 'Stay there,' I said to the rats. 'Quiet.' I closed the door and crossed to the opposite side of the street. The light was still on. It had a funny sort of permanent look as if it would never go out. I stood there gazing and waiting. Everything else went out of my head. I saw just the light. I felt it drawing me to itself. So must a moth feel. But I didn't move. My feet were held to the pavement as if both they and it were power-fully magnetised.

I was roused from my trance by a yell. A man was standing close beside my car. His head and shoulders were just coming out from the window at the driver's seat. Had I left it open? I had certainly left the car unlocked, but that was deliberate. I wouldn't have time to unlock it later when the critical moment arrived. The man cursed two or three times rather indistinctly. He kicked at the car wheels and went off mumbling. Obviously drunk. Probably he'd been fumbling about looking for something to steal and got his hand bitten by Ben. Teach him a lesson. I drew back a little into deeper shadow. I didn't want to be seen by anyone, drunk or sober. I watched the drunk man anxiously as he lurched slowly up the street. Every now and then he stopped and seemed to suck his finger, but the street was too dark for me to be sure what he was doing. He stopped again at the light of the shop and stayed there for a long time. I expect he was examining his wounded finger, but I can't be sure. I waited in horrible suspense. Suppose Mr. Shop-keeper came out and Mr. Drunk told him what had happened. That might spoil everything. Not that I think Mr. Shopkeeper would have listened for very long to Mr. Drunk. They wouldn't have been sympathetic personalities.

Mr. Drunk went on. For a little it seemed as if he couldn't get round the corner. Then he managed it. Just in time. The light in the shop went out.

I sprinted across the road and flung open the two doors of the car nearest to the pavement. 'Out!' I ordered. Rats came pouring out. I could see them by the inside light of the car. They were like a brown river. They made a soft continuous thudding, a sort of murmur, as they jumped down on to the pavement. 'Stop!' I said. They stopped. Ben had enough rats by this time—two-fifty, three hundred. I was going to need the rest myself. I jumped into the car and closed the door. 'Stay there!' I told Ben. 'When I whistle, come.'

I started the engine and reversed the car diagonally across the street till I was beside the chalk mark on the warehouse wall. I stopped there and switched off the engine. I opened the doors nearest the pavement. 'Out!' I told the remaining rats. 'Under the car. Wait!'

I paused and watched the shop again. No light. No sound. Surely he was taking longer than usual. Some sort of sound, perhaps a creak made faint by the distance. A scraping noise. The door must have sunk on its hinges. He had to give a tug to get it open. I whistled, a piercing whistle, distinct, but not very loud. The old man came out and slammed the door with a bang. It must be self-locking. He didn't use any keys. He had his bag with him and began his usual shuffling walk along the pavement.

I glanced quickly towards the other end of the street. I could just make out that Ben and his party were on the move. It looked as if the pavement were slowly creeping forward to meet the old man. I glanced back at *him*. He was coming on regardless.

I dived into the car again and took out my rat-head mask. I kept myself well hidden by the car as I put it on. Plenty of time. I adjusted it so that I could see out quite comfortably. Remaining crouched beside the car I watched the old man and Ben's party of rats approach each other. I didn't want him to see them too soon, not in fact till he was almost among them—and it was going to work out that way. I chuckled to myself—silently, of course. What a shock he'd get! Nearer and nearer. As he came level with the car and began to pass it I slipped round to the back. He *was* past it. 'Now!' I whispered to the rats underneath the car. 'Follow me!' I tip-toed across the road and they came after, their soft footfalls making only the faintest stir that no deaf old man could hear.

The old man stopped. He gave a funny little grunt. 'Huh-huh, what's this?' He'd noticed Ben's lot, but he didn't seem really frightened. He looked for a moment, gave another little grunt. 'Better go back.' He turned round and began to shuffle back the way he had come, slightly faster perhaps, but not much. He wasn't panicking. He saw that the rats weren't moving very fast.

I had come right across the road and was pressed close against the wall on the same side as the old man. He didn't see me, but almost immediately he saw the second party of rats. 'Dear me,' he exclaimed—a mild old voice. Slightly agitated, you would say, nothing more. He began to run. He wasn't very good at running, but he would get through all right. It wasn't part of my plan to corner him. I had already diverted the second lot of rats so that they weren't actually on the pavement, but running along in the gutter hemming him in. He would have to pass close to the wall, close to me.

It all worked out exactly. He came stumbling along looking at the ground. First he caught sight of my feet. Another human being. Someone who'd help him. His eyes travelled up my body. Then he saw the rat face grinning at him. He gave a sort of gasp. It was at this instant that I snatched his bag. Snatched is the wrong word—relieved him of it. He made no fight. It almost dropped from his fingers. I thought he was going to faint. For a moment I was even afraid that he might drop dead at my feet. But he didn't. He staggered on. These old businessmen are tougher than you'd think. Well I'm glad. I didn't want to hurt him. He's done me no harm, only good.

'Back to the car,' I told the rats. Myself I stayed on the pavement to watch the old man. He kept running. I wondered would he go back to the shop to telephone, but no. He couldn't risk the delay of perhaps fumbling with his key, having to fight with the door. He went on round the corner and disappeared in the same direction as the drunk. I hurried back to the car. Nearly all the rats were in. I gave a helping hand to the last few. I took off my mask, put the bag in the car, got in, drove home. No trouble. Do it again any time.

£845. Best night's work so far!

The papers are full of it. In the office no one could talk of anything else. People in offices spend a lot of time talking. The old man is in hospital suffering from shock, but his condition isn't serious. I'm glad. I wouldn't like him to die on my account. Probably in the long run the fright will do him good.

Jones as usual is the great expert. He stood in the middle of the office and talked to the Book-keeper in a loud voice, so that the whole staff could hear. He knows all about the rats. One of these days he's going to know a bit more.

Everyone I think is a little frightened. Before today I don't think most people really believed that Ratman existed. Now almost everyone believes in him. Tonight I bought an evening paper, a thing I don't usually do. On the way home in the bus I read an article— 'What is Ratman?', complete with artist's impression. Actually the artist's impression isn't bad except that I'm given claws instead of hands. I mean it's quite like the mask. I looked round the bus. Nearly everyone was reading the same article. I laughed sardonically, but silently. If they just knew that Ratman was sitting beside them on the bus.

The old man has left hospital and been interviewed by newspaper reporters. He has given a detailed description of Ratman, which confirms the artist's impression in yesterday's paper. The creature has the legs and trunk of a man, but face, head and claws like a monster rat.

I couldn't resist buying a paper again tonight. There is an article on monstrous births.

Incidentally when I got home I found last night's paper spread out all over the floor of the dining room. I left it in the dining room all right, but I certainly didn't leave it like that. So far as I know nobody has a key of the house but myself. There was no sign of any door or window having been forced. I can only conclude that the rats for some reason got hold of the paper and spread it over the floor. But why? There doesn't seem any sense in it.

Still front page headline news. All the national dailies feature the old man's account of his experiences. Two of them also have an interview with the drunk. One of them gives about a quarter of a column to the drunk, headed, 'Has Ratman a Car?' The funny thing is that the old man didn't see the car and denies emphatically that there was any car in the street. But both papers have a photograph of the drunk with a bandage on his finger. It's clever how both papers manage to convey that the drunk *was* drunk without actually saying so. They do it by treating Ratman's car as a sort of joke.

All this of course suits *me*. Confusion worse confounded. The more muddled everyone gets about Ratman the better. The girl and I pore over the papers together at lunch-time. She has taken to bringing a vacuum flask full of soup into the office every day, which we share. She won't let me pay anything.

Again last night's newspaper spread over the floor. I don't understand it.

I have been trying to think of something I could give the girl as a sort of return for the soup. I don't like accepting the soup every day and giving nothing back. And I've got really fond of the soup and wouldn't like to refuse it.

At last I decided to consult the Book-keeper. I told him that I would like to give the girl some small gift say once a week or once a fortnight, but that I couldn't think of even a first gift, let alone a whole series. It's lucky I did consult him. He has put me off the whole idea. He says it would be tantamount to a proposal of marriage. He knew of two chaps who had been caught in very similar circumstances. One had gone ahead with it, simply because he hadn't the nerve to do otherwise. The other had had letters from the girl's lawyers and had ended by paying through the nose to keep the thing out of the courts. So you never know where you are. 'Just remember,' the Book-keeper said, 'every spoonful of that soup you're walking a tight-rope. One slip and you're *in the soup*.' He thought that frightfully funny and nearly roared his head off. My laughter was more restrained. The thing is I like the soup. It's quite a change from my usual diet. In fact I'm putting on a little weight, but this may be partly due to having more money.

It has been noticed that Ratman always goes for cash. The theory now is that he's some sort of human monster so terrible that his birth was concealed. It is supposed that he has been brought up secretly, but that his relatives can no longer control him. Something like this is generally accepted, though there are all sorts of variations. I like the one about his mother being a lady of title.

Anyhow about ten days ago one of the local insurance brokers came out with an advertisement—'Insure your money against rats'—and now even the respectable companies have taken it up.

The rates don't really seem to me too dear. You can insure your money and valuables against theft or destruction by rats or Ratman. The premium for a thousand pound policy is ten pounds. The rate for smaller amounts is slightly higher. After great consultations between Jones and the Book-keeper the office has taken out a policy for a thousand which is more than we usually have in cash. Most business places are doing something similar. Some private people too. Major Robinson told me that he had, and asked was I going to. I said I was considering it. I would do it too, just for camouflage, only these insurance companies are great people for poking their noses in. They might want to inspect the 'Risk' as they call it. Lot of Nosey Parkers.

Another commercial side-issue from my activities has been a craze for Ratman masks. All the children are rushing about with them. Some of them seem almost identical with the one I've got.

All for the good of trade.

Jones Day draws near.

I am planning another raid for next week, but this doesn't mean I've forgotten Jones. I think of Socrates every day. Ben will never take his place. I still don't really like Ben. Now that I haven't Socrates I don't really like any of the rats. Sometimes I wish I'd never seen a rat.

The raid I'm planning now isn't financially necessary at the moment. Though the cost of keeping the rats is getting more and more as *they* get more and more, I've enough money to do for a long time to come. It's just I feel that I ought to have what's now called in business a planned cash flow. It would be bad policy to wait again till I'm really short and then do something desperate. Besides I think it's well to keep my hand in—and my nerve. I needn't pretend that I'm not very nervous at times. But I do like hearing people talking of Ratman and wondering what he'll do next. In secret I laugh and laugh. It's like being famous under a nom-de-plume.

The previous day's newspaper is on the floor every night now when I go home. I needn't comment on it any more, but it still strikes me as strange. The pages which are uppermost are always those which contain the latest articles or news items about the rats. You'd think someone came in every day and sat on the floor reading about them. But of course no one can get in—except the rats.

Jones Day draws nearer.

I'm just back from a reconnaissance. With a car the whole country is open to me. I don't see why I should confine my activities to one city. If I spread them round a bit the police are less likely to be able to trace me. 'Where will Ratman strike next?' they ask themselves. At least so the paper says. Not that I think the police have yet the slightest clue. Still some slip on my part might easily put them on my track. When we kill Jones it won't be a slip, but it may strike the police as more than a coincidence. The Marauder, tyres, death. Will they link them up? When he's dead they may even hear of his killing a rat in the Ladies and add that to the chain. If they get as far as that they'll be getting warm. In killing Jones I shall be taking the biggest risk yet. But Socrates shall be avenged at all costs.

The greater the risk the greater the precautions I must take. The centre of interest will change till Jones Day brings it back home with a bang.

Last night I carried out my first away raid. I followed more or less the same plan as with the old man, except that this time I got my victim at the gate of his own home. He got out of his car to open the gate leaving the money in the car. Ben saw to it that he didn't get back to the car and I attended to the money. I wore my rat-head mask, but I don't think anyone saw me. I prefer not to be seen. The disguise has been a good one so far, but if I'm seen too often, someone, sometime, is going to realise that it *is* a disguise. At present everyone still believes I am some kind of deformed monster.

The police have warned the public to look out for a man with a club-foot. Why a club-foot? I am completely mystified, but of course it is all to the good.

Another raid on the twin city. Pretty good, but nothing like my snatch from the old man. I don't think I was seen.

I'm putting off Jones Day for a month or two. I'm creating a false sense of security in the home town.

My policy is paying off. The papers report that the demand for rat insurance has eased off here while it's still increasing in the sister-city.

All sorts of theories in the papers. 'Have the Rats Migrated?' and so on, but there's still a good deal of support for the 'Ratman has-a-car' school.

Had a very near shave tonight. I was going into the sister-city for a look-around. Not a raid. Just a look-around with an eye to future business. And I ran into a police road-block. I had Ben in the car with me. So I immediately shoved him into one of the glove cupboards in the dash and locked it. Then I sat back and prepared for the worst.

A policeman came up very apologetic. 'Do you mind, Sir, if we have a look over your car?'

'Not at all,' I said. 'Go ahead. What are you looking for?' Of course I was sweating.

The policeman became more embarrassed than ever. 'Rats,' he answered, looking thoroughly ashamed of himself. 'You don't have any rats in the car.'

'I hope not,' I told him. 'If you find any you might put them out.'

'This is a queer sort of arrangement you've got in the boot,' he remarked presently, his voice coming through the back seat.

'It is indeed,' I agreed. 'I don't know what the idea of it is. I got the car second-hand and it was like that when I got it. I think a builder or a painter or something must have had it before and used that hole for carrying a ladder or something.'

I heard the boot bang. He came round to the front and opened the glove cupboard on the passenger side. It wasn't locked. There was nothing in it but a pair of gloves—rubber gloves, strangely enough.

He leaned over and pointed to the glove-cupboard on my side. 'What's in there?'

'I haven't the faintest notion,' I told him. 'It was locked when I got it and I've never been able to get a key that will open it. It may be full of rats for all I know, but if they're not dead they must be pretty hungry for they'll have been in there a long time.'

He laughed and got out. 'Sorry for troubling you Sir. It's all this rat-caper. They're looking for these motoring rats, complete with Ratman if they can find him. A bit silly, it strikes me, but we have to do what we're told.'

'That's all right officer. We've all got to do our duty, and where we'd be without the police I don't like to think. Probably lying in bed with our throats cut.'

Nice touch that. But heavens alive I was sweating so much I wonder he didn't smell me.

No more raids for the time being. Jones Day postponed indefinitely. The police are altogether too active. I'll have to lie low for a bit. Fortunately I've enough money to do for a good while.

Saturday. So I arrived home at lunch-time. Something made me look through the dining room window before going into the house. There was Ben crouched in the middle of a newspaper spread out on the floor. His head was cocked on one side. You'd have thought he was reading the paper with his right eye. Alternatively he might have been watching a fly on the ceiling with his left eye. When I got in he had gone. I didn't see him again till after lunch.

The newspapers are saying that people carrying large sums of money ought to be armed. One of them has a heading, 'Ratman dead or alive.'

I hear there's a great increase in the sale of revolvers and automatic pistols.

An extraordinary thing has happened. At least it seems extraordinary after all these years. Uncle has actually died. And he has left a fortune. To me. Well, about forty-five thousand pounds at the present rate for the Canadian dollar. It's funny. I go home thinking nothing in particular and there's this letter waiting for me. I wonder what it is—vaguely, not particularly interested. Then I read it, my eyes popping out of my head. At first I can hardly believe it. It must be a dream or a hoax. But The Royal Trust Company, Executors and Trustees, 10039 Jasper Avenue, Edmonton, Canada, wouldn't hoax anyone. I read the letter about fifty times. Gradually I come to believe it. I am rich.

I don't think I'll tell anybody.

I have known that I am rich for just over twenty-four hours. So far my wealth has given me little pleasure, though I would hate to be poor again. I lay awake all last night, too excited to sleep. It wasn't pleasurable excitement. Strange to say I was worried—and I'm still worried. I don't know what to do with my money. Today in the office I couldn't concentrate on my work and made several stupid mistakes.

Of course I haven't got the money yet. There are several things I have to do. The Royal Trust Company suggests that I should consult a solicitor, but I know very well what solicitors are—leeches.

After all, I have told the girl, and I'm going to tell Jones. What's the good of having money if you can't get any pleasure out of it? Telling about it is the only way I can get any pleasure out of mine in the meantime.

The girl was delighted. It was lunch-time and we were alone together in the Cash Office. She burst into a sort of laugh and gave my arm a squeeze with both her hands. 'Oh! I'm so glad,' she exclaimed. 'Now you'll be able to do anything you like.'

The reason I'm going to tell Jones is to annoy him. Anything I have Jones thinks ought to be his. He's been scheming for years to get hold of my house. He's got a sort of chip on his shoulder about Father. He wants to be equal to Father, and in some funny way he can't feel he is so long as he doesn't live in Father's house. In the same way he'll want to get hold of my money.

Everything has quieted down. There hasn't been a thing in the papers for ages. I mean about rats or Ratman. In a way I quite miss it. I liked to know people were talking about me. I almost feel lonely.

Today in the office I remarked to the girl, sort of casually, 'It's funny, isn't it? You never hear anything about Ratman these days.'

For a moment she looked quite puzzled. Then she said, 'Oh that's the man that was supposed to go about with the rats, wasn't it? He was supposed to have something wrong with him, be deformed or something.'

'That's right,' I told her, quite pleased to think that my exploits hadn't been quite forgotten.

Next moment she spoiled it all, or very nearly. 'Oh I never believed in him,' she declared. 'I don't think there ever was any Ratman. The papers made it all up. At any rate it was greatly exaggerated.'

Fortunately I remembered that silence is golden. 'Sic transit gloria mundi,' I murmured to myself. That and, 'Dulce et decorum est pro patria mori,' is about all the Latin I know. Not much use for Dulcie in this country just at the moment, but she'll be at it again one of these days.

The gist of all this is that Jones Day could be any time. Of course I don't know what the police are thinking or what they're up to, but I don't see that the chances are ever going to get any better. There's bound to be some risk whenever I do it.

Recently I have been doing a good deal of motoring at night sometimes by myself, sometimes with the girl. No rats on board. In fact I've given her some quite decent dinners. But that's not the point. The point is to make sure there are no road-blocks any more, that the police aren't searching cars. I'll keep on checking till Jones Day minus one, Jones Eve I might call it.

Jones Day is fixed. It has fixed itself really, in a rather strange way, for the Friday after next. Today is also a Friday. This evening when I was about to put away the cash preparatory to going home I suddenly realised I was short of money myself—not permanently short. I've more than a thousand hidden round the house at home. But I'd promised to take the girl for a run in the car, and of course I knew she'd expect me to stand her a meal as well. And the car needed petrol. So I took a fiver out of the office cash and scribbled a little note 'I O U £5' and shoved it in. The Book-keeper happened to be watching. 'I wouldn't do that if I were you,' he said. 'You know Mr. Jones always checks the cash on Friday nights. I wouldn't put it past him to burn your I O U and say you're a fiver short. He's after your blood, you know.'

'Well you're my witness. He'll only be showing himself up if he tries anything like that.'

'I wouldn't do it all the same. He wouldn't like it. He'd say you'd no right to borrow from the cash, and so do I.'

Of course I had to put it back. It was a nuisance. It meant going out home first and then of course the girl wanted to come in. I didn't let her. I told her that the house wasn't in a fit state for any girl to come into, and nor it is. In fact I made her stay in the car at the gate. She was quite sniffy about it, but I was standing no nonsense.

'So that's what Jones does on Friday nights,' I remarked.

'What?' the girl asked.

I explained.

'You'd think he might trust you after all these years.'

'Our Mr. Jones trusts nobody.'

'I suppose he knows nobody should trust him and judges everyone else by himself.' The girl has come to quite my way of thinking about Jones.

'As if I'd want to touch the firm's money. You'd think I'd none coming of my own.'

And it was then the idea came to me. The thought of Jones, sitting there all by himself counting the money, put it into my head. Why not kill Jones on a night when he's got plenty of money to count, and get the money as well. Before that I hadn't even thought of money in connection with killing Jones.

I took a little sideways look at the girl to see if she was watching me, but she was looking out of the window. I sometimes feel that if people are watching me they can maybe know what I'm thinking.

In our firm the staff are always paid on the last day of the month, and they're always paid in cash. This month the last day is a Saturday. Saturday is the half-day with us, and when the month ends on a Saturday I always draw the money for the salaries on the Friday. So on the Friday after next Jones will have quite a lot of money to count. Perhaps I'll draw a little extra by mistake.

Today I told Jones about my money. He was very impressed. A cunning look immediately came into his eyes. I'm sure he began straight off to try to work out some scheme to get hold of part of it. Part of it! That'd be a first instalment. He'd want it all. But his first reaction was a sort of sly deference. And that'll go on till he manages to get hold of it or I lose it some other way. Not that I shall lose it. I'm not as stupid as he thinks. And whatever happens I'll make sure he doesn't get near any of it. It's funny the feeling he has for money. He respects anyone who's richer than he is, and when I get this money I should be a good deal richer than him.

One thing you can say about Jones. He's a fast worker. About twelve o'clock today he sent one of the typists—the one he calls his secretary—to the Cash Office with a message that he wanted to see me. Both the Book-keeper and the girl looked quite startled. Obviously they thought I was going to get the sack. I didn't. In fact I guessed pretty well what was in the wind. Of course getting the sack wouldn't matter to me financially any more, though it might upset my plans for Jones Day. The Book-keeper knows nothing of my new financial status. As I got up to go to Jones's office he came over and whispered, 'If Mr. Jones says anything it's nothing to do with me. I've always put in a good word for you when I could.'

I thanked him, but of course you never know what people really do say about you behind your back.

Jones smiled at me very affably and waved me to a comfortable chair. But he didn't offer me a cigarette, though he was smoking himself. Of course I don't smoke. *He* smokes like a fish. He waited till I was thoroughly settled. Then he started off, 'I've been giving some thought to this problem of yours.'

Of course I knew very well what he meant, but I pretended not to understand. I put on a puzzled expression. 'Problem?'

Jones looked slightly irritated, but he kept control of his temper in a way he would never have bothered to do before he heard about my money. 'The investment problem you consulted me about. This money you have coming to you.'

Of course I hadn't consulted him. I'd just told him about it. This was the artfulness of him and I found myself saying without really meaning to, 'Oh yes. I don't quite know what I ought to put it into.' And of course I don't. I've never had money to invest before. But I had no intention of taking Jones's advice.

Jones gave a long drag at his cigarette and then let out a great cloud of smoke. 'Of course you could put it into equities, spread it over really sound securities. You'd get four and a half to five per cent, depending on what you selected.'

'That's not a very high yield.'

'It's a shocking low yield, and not all that safe even so. Some of these high priced stocks can come a cropper just as quick as any others.'

'Oh yes,' I agreed vaguely, feeling that even if I didn't take Jones's advice I'd still quite a problem on my hands.

'And then there are Government stocks,' he went on. 'You can get a yield of six per cent there all right, but when you try to get your money out you'll probably find you won't be able to get as much out as you put in—and in any case what you do get will be *worth* less.'

He gave another long draw on his cigarette and I felt we were really getting near the point. 'It certainly is a problem,' I commented, just because I felt he expected me to say something, and I wanted to keep him going. I mean I wanted to find out what villainy he had thought up.

'Of course there are always *private* companies,' he said, letting the smoke clear a bit and giving me one of those quick, furtive looks that now always make me think of Ben.

I've known him like this before—all over himself to be helpful, but with deep dark schemes of his own. Not so deep either. You could see through them with a pitchfork. 'Sometimes it's easier to get into private companies than to get out of them,' I remarked, remembering Father's shares and what Jones had got them at. He was the only buyer, though we heard afterwards that someone else might have been interested.

'Ah yes,' he answered. 'I suppose you're thinking of my position, saddled with a lot of shares there's no market in, but I couldn't let you and your mother starve.'

I gaped at the absolute brazenness of it, and he went on without turning a hair, 'I always had a great respect for your father and a great affection for him. In the last years we were very close and I like to feel that I lightened his burden more than somewhat.'

At this I could only gasp. I'm sure Father would never have

trusted him an inch. But I was longing to know what his scheme was.

'What I was going to suggest was *this* company.' He held up his hand as if I had been going to interrupt him. 'No. I'm not going to ask you to buy back shares. We are both fully aware of the disadvantages of that. What I had in mind was more in the nature of a partnership. As you know the position of this business has improved very considerably since I took control, but I have been a good deal hampered at times by lack of capital. We could have made twice the money we have made. Now if you were to put in twenty thousand. . . .' He paused to see how I would take it.

Secretly I laughed to myself. Just as I'd expected, the first instalment. Two bites at the cherry—and as Churchill might have said, 'Some cherry!'

I said, 'What interest would I get?'

He rubbed his chin for a bit and then lit another cigarette. 'I thought perhaps we might manage participating up to twelve and a half per cent.'

I felt a little foolish. 'I don't quite know what you mean. I mean what participating means.'

He grinned. 'I'm inviting you to become my partner. We would enter into a partnership agreement whereby you would be assured of a share in the profits up to twelve and a half per cent on the amount you'd invested—twenty thousand, two thousand five hundred a year.'

I must confess it sounds awfully good and I still can't see the catch in it. I'm almost glad that the money hasn't come through yet. I believe I'd have handed it over to him there and then. But I remembered something. 'What security would I have?' I enquired.

'The best security in the world. The money'd still be there.'

'Do you mean you wouldn't use it? What good would it be to you if you didn't use it?'

'Of course we'd use it, but it would still be there in the form of goods and in money owed us by our customers.'

I thought the goods would be all right. Jones is a pretty shrewd buyer, but I wasn't so sure about our customers. Some of them seem pretty shaky. 'What about bad debts? If a customer went bust and didn't pay, would that be my money lost?'

Again he looked slightly irritated and I wondered if this was where the catch was. 'Of course bad debts are a risk, but they're a risk we run all the time. Over the last ten years our percentage of bad debts to turnover has been just over a quarter of one per cent. We reckon on a net profit on turnover of five per cent before tax, and we usually manage to turn our money just over three times in the year. That gives a profit of slightly over fifteen per cent on capital invested. So I'm putting you on to a good thing.'

It certainly seemed so, but I remembered that it was the same business that Father had owned, and he hadn't found it so profitable in his latter years. I was almost afraid to mention this. At times I feel rather frightened of Jones, but I plucked up courage. 'Father didn't find it such a good thing.'

'Your father didn't turn his money often enough. He'd have stuff lying eighteen months at a time, some of it nearly unsaleable. Often he'd have to take less than cost to get rid of it. That's where the money was lost.' He got up suddenly. 'Well you can think it over. Let me know when the money comes through. Now you'd better get back to your work.'

I hurried out feeling that he'd suddenly got fed up with me. There's no doubt Jones is an efficient businessman, and I suppose you'd say he doesn't suffer fools gladly, which means he's no time for people like me—because there's no doubt he considers me a fool. Perhaps I am from his point of view. Anyhow I left him feeling like a fool—very small in fact. I sort of shrank through the door of the Cash Office, got over to my desk somehow and started in at my work as quickly as I could.

The girl was over to me like a shot. 'He hasn't sacked you has he?'

'No, no. Nothing like that.'

'Well I'm glad of that at any rate,' said the Book-keeper. He's got ears about a mile long.

'Well what did he want then?' the girl demanded. She's not very polite sometimes. 'You were in there quite a while.'

'He just wanted a little talk,' I answered nonchalantly. 'A matter he wanted to discuss.'

She got quite huffed. 'Oh if you're going to be snooty about it you can just keep it to yourself—and if you do get the sack I'm sure I don't care.'

I wouldn't have minded this if it hadn't been for the Book-keeper. I could see him laughing away to himself fit to bust. He didn't make a sound, so that the girl, who was facing the other way didn't even realise that she was making a fool of herself. The silly thing was that of course I meant to tell her all about it. It was the Book-keeper I was keeping in the dark because he doesn't know about my money. I was meaning to talk to the girl at lunch-time, but I didn't get a chance. She must have had her lunch in the Ladies. She didn't even give me any soup. I've come to count on that soup. I mean I allow for it when I'm packing my lunch-box at home. The result was I didn't have enough to eat and rumbled a bit during the afternoon. I always do rumble if I don't get my meals at the proper time and enough of them. And of course soup's a very filling thing. Leaving it out if you've made allowances for it makes quite a hole. I don't know whether the girl heard my rumbles or not, but later on she looked as if she was sorry and at going-home time she said, 'Goodnight,' in a very friendly way.

I've told the girl all about my interview with Jones. I had her out in the car again. She's sorry she was cross. She thought I was trying to keep secrets from her. She never thought we might have talked about something I didn't want the Book-keeper to know.

She thinks that if once Jones got his hands on the money I'd never see it again, capital or interest.

'Of course there'd always be the other half. He only suggested putting twenty thousand into the business. I'd have the other twenty.'

'*He*'d have it before you were a year older. I don't know why you've gone so soft about him all of a sudden. He just has to be half-civilised to you for ten or fifteen minutes and you're ready to eat out of his hand.'

All I'd said was that he'd really seemed to be trying to be help-ful. Only 'Seemed.' I didn't say he was. And it was quite true. He did *seem* to be trying to be helpful. I was amused. Little she knew. Me being soft with Jones. Jones Day is only a week away. However there was no harm in fostering the impression. 'Oh maybe he's not such a bad soul after all,' I remarked in a nice syrupy voice. 'I expect he really wants to be a help. Perhaps he feels we had a bit of a rough deal the time Father died and thinks he sees a way of making it up to me, perhaps helping himself a bit at the same time.'

'Helping himself,' she said, 'full-stop. Don't you let him have a penny.'

Of course I don't intend to. Anyhow there won't be time.

Jones Eve. Approaching midnight. All my preparations are made. This time tomorrow Jones should be dead.

I think it will be quite simple really. I'll come into the office and find him checking the cash, trying to catch me out, making sure I haven't been pinching a bit on the quiet, hoping I have. . . . I'll pretend that I've come to talk a bit more about investing my money, but I'll have the rod he killed Socrates with. He'll wonder what *that's* for.

Now it *is* Jones Day. I must have gone to sleep for a little in my chair. I thought I was too excited to sleep. I'd better go up to bed all the same—even though I probably won't sleep once I'm there. Still I ought to get my clothes off and rest. I'll need all my wits about me tomorrow—I mean this evening.

It's done. Oh God.

I can't possibly sleep. I might as well write it down. It may stop me trembling . . . start right from the . . . start right . . . if I start right from the beginning. . . .

If only I had a drink of whisky. They say . . . I sold the only bottle we had . . . never been opened . . . the time I'd no money.

Funny no rats, left them all behind.

I suddenly remembered Mother's wardrobe. I always had an idea she'd something there. It was only a very small bottle, with about two mouthfuls left in the bottom. But it's done the trick.

The thing that was worrying me was the car. I thought if I left the car outside the office it might look a bit conspicuous. I mean there aren't many people or cars about those streets at night and a policeman might just note the number, just in case. But of course I'd forgotten about Jones's car. And then I had a bit of luck. Inspiration you might call it. I tried all the doors and he'd left one open. Well. I simply transferred the rats to Jones's car and went away and left mine in a park. Then I came back and let them straight into the office. I didn't see a soul either time and Jones never heard the door opening or shutting. I could see that his light was on. I tip-toed down the passage and got the metal rod. It's always in the corner behind the meter-box. I don't know why. That's where the boy got it from that time. Jones can't have heard a thing.

I opened the door of *his* office suddenly. He looked up. You wouldn't even have thought he was very surprised. But he must have been. The money was all round him on Father's big desk, neat piles of coins, bundles of notes, still there. Didn't take any. Might be blood on them.

I stood there looking at him, the rod upright in my hand. Like Moses.

'Hullo,' he said. 'What do you want?' I think he thought I was drunk.

'I wanted to ask you about my money. It's come.' This is true. I received the first payment, a Banker's draft on account of income this morning.

'I think you'd better leave it till tomorrow,' he suggested. 'I'm busy at the moment.'

'I wanted to get you when you were alone,' I told him. 'There'll be other people here tomorrow.'

I kept the door open and all the time we were talking the rats were slipping in round my feet. But he wasn't looking at my feet. 'Does it matter?' he asked.

'It matters to me,' I answered. 'I wouldn't want a lot of people about.' And I couldn't help smiling, because he didn't know yet why I didn't want a lot of people about.

'I've come for revenge,' I explained.

'Revenge for what?' I thought he sounded annoyed and that perhaps he was beginning to feel a little frightened.

'Revenge for the death of Socrates.'

'Who the hell's Socrates?' Obviously he hadn't a notion, but I'd got him worried.

'They made him drink hemlock.'

'What's that when it's at home?' He was trying to be jocular. Humour the drunk man.

'It's a deadly poison.'

Just then he happened to glance down. 'Oh God!' he said. 'Look at the rats.'

'Yes,' I responded. 'Look at the rats. Lots of rats. Not just one any more. Have a good look at them. Look at the rats.' I pointed the rod at him and made passes with it in the air, as if I was fencing.

He was watching me very intently and suddenly a sort of look of understanding seemed to break over his face. 'You wouldn't be Ratman, by any chance?' he enquired.

I let out a loud laugh. 'Yes. I'm Ratman.' I shouted. 'You didn't think there was a ratman, did you? But I've been Ratman all along. From the very beginning. And Socrates was a rat and you killed him with this rod.'

He gave a bit of a snigger. 'Oh so that was Socrates was it. It's nice to know.'

'Oh very nice,' I agreed sarcastically. 'And it was very nice the way you killed him with this rod. What's more, he was my friend. The best friend I ever had. The only friend I ever had since they poisoned my dog.'

In spite of being able to be sarcastic I was in quite a state. All the humiliations I'd suffered from him over the years boiled up in me. Oh how I hated him. I gave him a poke with the rod. It wasn't a very hard poke, but it was meant to hurt and I'm sure it did. He gave a sort of yelp. He tried to push back his chair, but he couldn't. The legs caught in the carpet or something. His yelp instead of making me feel sorry for him set me on fire. I remembered Socrates and Jones poking at him with this very rod. Now I had Jones at my mercy. He couldn't get out of the chair. Every time he tried I put in another quick, rapier-like thrust. Of course his clothes were saving him. I couldn't have got through and drawn blood and it didn't occur to me to go for his face and neck. I was panting with passion and excitement. It was hard work.

I didn't notice him getting his hand into the right-hand pocket of his jacket. Suddenly there was a crash and an explosion. I suppose it must have been the other way round. I heard glass falling behind me. I drew back with a start. I got a fright. My rage went just like that. I was immediately cool again. I realised what had happened. Jones had taken the advice the police and the papers were giving—anyone working with money at night to carry a

revolver. Only it was an automatic pistol of some sort he was pulling out of his pocket. He'd tried to shoot me with it in his pocket
and missed. As soon as he could get his aim properly he would
shoot again and kill me this time. I was frightened. I didn't know
what to do. Instinctively I took another step back. I saw the pistol
come up. The electric light glinted on something blue in the metal
of the barrel. He had difficulty steadying it. 'Drop that tube,' he
ordered.

His voice was shaky, but I dropped it. I found myself licking my
lips. They tasted salty.

'Put up your hands.'

Up went my hands. My eyes were fixed on the barrel of the
automatic. It was as if I was hypnotised.

'Turn and face . . .'

I was beginning to turn when Bang! Crash!

Something brown was fixed on his hand. The pistol went off
again and I heard the bullet smash into some wooden panelling
just below the level of the glass to my right. The pistol fell on to
the carpet. Jones jumped up.

'Damn and bloody hell!' He was shaking his hand and after a
moment Ben dropped off. But there were rats all over him now.
He kept brushing at his back and the collar of his jacket, first with
one hand then the other. The blood was dripping from his right
hand and leaving streaks of blood on his clothes.

He came staggering round the desk towards the door and I
retreated in front of him through the door and into the passage.
He was frightening. I stood in the passage between the door of his
office and the street door. I had calmed a little and regained my
wits. I thought he would make for the street door and that I would
have to try and stop him. My rage had quite gone. I didn't even
want to kill him any more. I felt somehow that Socrates was sufficiently avenged. I even felt an inclination to help the man against
the rats.

He came lurching out and saw me. His face was ghastly. I
suppose the sight of me turned him. He went the opposite way
towards the door of the yard. There were three or four rats on his
back. They were through his jacket. I saw the white of his shirt. In
another moment they'd be tearing the skin from his back.

He started a sort of half-run. I suppose it was the most he could manage. And then I saw that there were more rats between him and the yard-door. They were coming under the yard-door. These couldn't be my rats. I hadn't brought so many rats with me. Jones saw them too. He turned to the right and made for the stairs. The stairs lead up to the lofts. He jumped up the first few steps. Then stopped and tore off his jacket. He threw it down to the foot of the stairs where the rats were already approaching. He bent down and brushed two or three rats off his trousers. He kicked at them furiously for a moment or two. I think he must have killed them. Then he went on up the stairs. His shirt was torn and through it I could see that his back was bleeding.

I wondered if he'd thought of any way to escape. I couldn't let him escape. And I knew there were several possibilities open to him. He might open one of the upstairs windows, lean out and yell. There was a chance that someone might hear him. Or no one might hear him. The whole district was usually pretty well deserted at night, except for the odd person working late. His only chance would be some such person going home, or perhaps a policeman on patrol. And what could one person do? Call the fire-brigade perhaps. That wouldn't save him. The rats would catch up in three or four minutes at the most. But it might sink me. He might have time to shout out who Ratman was.

All this went through my mind in seconds. Ben's contingent of rats was already coming out of Jones's office and starting to run down the passage. 'Come on,' I shouted. 'After him. Hurry.' I ran to the foot of the stairs taking care not to tread on the rats Jones had shaken off. He had killed two with his kicks and there was another writhing and screaming on the bottom step. I jumped over it and went up the stairs three at a time.

I got to the first loft and saw Jones a flight ahead of me. He was turning on lights as he went. At the second loft he was still a flight ahead of me. Perhaps he had even gained a little. He was fitter than I would have imagined. I reached the third loft and heard his footsteps, clear of the stairs, running across the fourth. The fourth loft was the top and it had no windows opening on to the street. So he wasn't going to try that. The fire-escape? But that only led back into the yard, and there'd be rats in the yard. I heard him dragging something across the floor. I got to the top and saw. He'd got a ladder and was putting it beneath one of the skylights. Really it was his best chance. He'd get away over the roof-tops, perhaps find another skylight and get down and out through another building.

Though I was out of breath and panting I was thinking very clearly. I mustn't get into a fight with Jones. If there was a fight he might mark me. If, for instance, I had a black eye in the morning someone would be sure to report it to the police. And the police would investigate. I couldn't risk even being suspected.

So for a moment I hung back. I watched Jones get the ladder into position and start to go up it. He had his back to me. I began to tiptoe across the floor. But he heard me. 'Don't try anything or I'll kick your face in,' he warned me. I made a grab at the bottom of the ladder, but he came down a rung or two and nearly got me with his foot. I ran back to the top of the stairs. Up he went again and began to wrestle with the bar of the skylight. It seemed to be stuck or something. I could hear him panting. I advanced again and began to circle round warily, keeping well out of range of his feet. I thought if I kept the ladder between him and me he might have more difficulty in kicking me. But as soon as he saw me there he began to come down again. I think he maybe thought he'd fight it out with me first and then make his escape. So I ran back to the stairhead. 'The rats will be here any moment,' I said. 'They're on the third loft already.'

I didn't know where they were. He hesitated a moment and went back up the ladder. This time he got on better. Whatever was jamming the skylight came free. I saw him begin to raise it.

I ran back past the ladder. He must have either seen or heard me, but this time he paid no attention. I didn't risk bending down to tug the ladder with my hands. I knew he might have come down on top of me in seconds. Instead I ran back again towards the stair-head, and as I passed I gave a hard kick at the bottom of the ladder. The side I kicked slipped a little. Not much, but Jones lost his balance and had to hold on with both hands. The skylight dropped down with a bang. I came back and kicked again. The ladder began to slip sideways. Jones was obviously powerless to kick me now. I grabbed the bottom of the ladder and pulled. It came away from the floor. The top slipped off the beam it was propped against. I let go and ran back to the top of the stairs as Jones and the ladder crashed to the floor.

I waited there, watching. If Jones came after me I would run downstairs again till we met the rats coming up. Jones didn't pick himself up very quickly. He was groaning a bit. At last he made an effort. He tried to help himself up with one arm, but it didn't seem to be working properly. He gave a little cry and lay still for a few moments. Then he tried again. This time he was successful. He staggered to his feet and stood looking at me. 'Why not let me go?' he suggested. 'I never done you any harm.'

'Because you'd tell on me. You'd tell the police. I'd be put in gaol.'

'I'd promise not to tell anyone.'

'But you wouldn't keep your promise. You've broken other promises—and you wouldn't even feel bound by this one. You'd say it was a promise to a madman to save your life and didn't count.'

'I'd keep it,' he said.

I knew he wouldn't. Who would in the circumstances?

I heard a sort of soft rustling sound, a sound I recognised—the sound of the feet of many rats. I looked down. There they were, a column of them, about five abreast. They were on the third loft just coming up to the stairs.

'What are you looking at?' Jones asked.

I was sorry for him, but I couldn't help making a joke of it. 'Our friends,' I answered.

'Oh God! Are they here?'

'They will be in a minute.'

'Please let me go. We're both men after all, and I've always done my best for you. I did keep you in your job, when you asked me to.'

'No.'

'Have mercy.'

'No.'

He tried to prop up the ladder again. I watched him. He couldn't manage it with only one arm working. I stood aside to make way for the rats. 'Tear him up,' I whispered softly. It was the only thing I *could* do. He went on bending over the ladder, trying to get it up, till the first rat jumped on his back. Then he straightened up and tried to knock it off.

I turned and slipped away down the stairs. I didn't want to see any more. I could only go down slowly feeling my way. There were rats on every step and I was careful not to stand on any of them. They were hopping up a step at a time, a long, unending column of them.

I don't know how long it took me to get to the first loft. But it was when I was there that the screaming became really loud. There are open hatchways on every loft for lowering goods into the yard. I stopped beside one of these, because I guessed what was going to happen.

There was a rattle of feet across the top loft and then a still louder scream. Jones jumped out of the top loft. I only got a glimpse of him as he fell past me, but he screamed all the way to the ground. I think he was covered with rats when he fell. If so he must have killed some when he hit the yard. The scream stopped when he hit the yard, as if it had been cut off with a knife.

I switched on the loading light and looked down. The yard was swarming with rats. Jones must have flattened quite a few when he landed. For the first time I felt a little frightened of the rats. Where on earth had they all come from?

For a moment the rats near Jones didn't move. His sudden arrival had frozen them. But the rats a little distance from him went on scurrying to and fro as if nothing had happened. Suddenly they all swarmed over him. He was hidden by rats. They were tearing him to pieces. But he wasn't dead. He moved. You'd have sworn that for an instant he almost tried to sit up.

I didn't watch any longer. I wanted to get away. I went downstairs to the office. There didn't seem to be rats in the office any longer except a few dead ones at the foot of the stairs. I felt I wanted to go home. I did think of Ben and the rats I'd brought with me. If I called them would they come or were they too engrossed in tearing Jones to pieces? First I would get them into Jones's car. Then I'd get my car and transfer them from one to the other. But there were far more rats now than just the ones I had brought. What if they all decided to come?

And then I thought, why bring any of them? And just as quickly as that I made my decision. I wouldn't. I'd had enough of rats. I'd just go home without them. All I had to do was walk out of the front door of the office and I'd never see them again. They'd never get home by themselves. It's five miles from home to the office.

I was so taken with this idea that I was about to walk out of the front door then and there. Only I remembered I hadn't locked up. Well nowadays there's hardly any locking up to be done. In the old days it was quite a complicated business. Now all that's necessary is to shut the safes, turn off the lights and slam the front door after you. There was only one safe open. The one where the money's kept. When I went to shut it I remembered all the money in Jones's office. It seemed funny shutting the safe leaving all that lying about. And it suddenly stuck me I shouldn't be locking the safe, because I wasn't supposed to be there at all. So I left it open. But from force of habit I went to the electric meter cupboard and switched off all the lights. It was only when I got to the door a second time that I realised that the light would have to be left on. I took a kind of pull on myself. I was really in a daze. I said to myself, 'Wake up. You've got to make it look as if there'd been no one here but Jones and the rats.' So I went back and turned the lights on again. Then I went to Jones's office and wiped both handles of the door with my handkerchief just in case I'd left any fingerprints. I spotted the metal rod and put it back in the corner by the meter-box. I wiped the main switch in the meter-box, which I'd touched when I turned the lights out, and when I'd put them on again afterwards. I didn't touch the safe. It would have been almost bound to have had my fingerprints on it in any case, from my ordinary work in the daytime. The fingerprints of the whole staff would be scattered all round the office. It might look suspicious if there were none on the safe.

I stood still for a moment, forcing myself to think coolly. There was nothing else I should do. I went to the door once more. I stood inside listening carefully. No sound of footsteps on the pavement. I opened the door cautiously, looked up and down and slipped out. No one about. I went to the car park, got my car and drove home. Funny I didn't begin to shake till I was safe inside the house.

Time the Great Healer. Though less than twenty-four hours have passed I am almost my normal self. When I went up to bed last night I was sick. I think in some strange way that may have done me good. It took my mind off. . . . No good. If I'm not careful I shall be sick again. The thing is to forget. Forget there ever were any rats.

The most difficult moment was when I went into the office. As it was Saturday none of the female staff was there. Which was lucky. Females notice more than men. I was still feeling pretty awful, but I didn't want to show it. I had to go into the office pretending I knew nothing. I don't usually buy a morning paper. I borrow the office one at lunch-time. But I knew it was in the papers. I'd seen the headlines when I was coming in on the bus.

'Rats Eat Man'

and

'Now, Man-Eating Rats.'

I was afraid they would notice I looked peculiar when I got into the office, and wonder *why*—if I *didn't* know what had happened. But I've a fair amount of self-control and I forced myself to look perfectly normal and unconcerned. In fact everyone was far too excited to notice how I looked—and once I knew officially, I could look as sick as I liked. It was only natural.

All they'd found of Jones was his skull. Licked pretty bare apparently. Eyes eaten out, cheeks gone, gums. . . . All they'd left was a little bit of scalp with hair clinging to it. This all according to the Book-keeper. Mrs. Jones rang the police when Hubby didn't come home and the police got the Book-keeper down to open up the place for them. Funny the hair being left. I mean he didn't have very much. It wouldn't go very far in lining nests. It seems there were still rats in the yard when the police arrived, but they didn't try to fight the police. They just bolted. You'd almost think Ben had been working to a plan of his own. They'd cleared away all the rat-corpses. It was as if they were trying to leave no sign at all. Even the blood was all licked up. All except a little under the skull where they found the bit of loose scalp with the hair on it. I'd never thought all that out. I hadn't meant them to go any further than killing Jones. Of course this is all to the good. No sign this time of any Ratman.

Monday. All the female staff in, surprisingly enough. Couldn't resist the gossip, I suppose. They gossiped all day. Then great panic at going-home time. No one wanted to be last out. As a matter of fact I was last, though I didn't mean to be. I found the others all waiting for me on the pavement. The girl said I was very brave. She says she and the rest of the females are going to give in their notice unless we move to new premises. Certainly no one is going to work late from now on. But I think that'll apply in nearly every business, not just ours.

I don't know what'll happen to our firm without Jones. I should think someone will try to carry it on. In a funny way I wish he was still alive. I miss him. I didn't really want to kill him exactly. But I had to. Hadn't I?

I wonder where Ben is now. Trying to walk it home. It's a long walk. I hope he never makes it.

All last night I had the most awful dreams. Sometimes Jones, sometimes Ben. . . .

It's funny to think that if I'd drowned old Ma Rat and her family away back at the beginning, as Mother wanted, I'd now be enjoying my new-found riches without a care in the world. Mother knew best. Now I'm going to do what I should have done then. All the adult male rats went off to the Jones affair. All the females not actually looking after litters, or just about to litter, went with them—and all the young rats of both sexes old enough to run about. The only rats left here are half-a-dozen nursing mothers—plus litters of course—and three or four more expecting next week. I'm going to drown them all on Saturday afternoon.

I'm working out how to do it. I don't think it will be difficult.

The greatest Rat Hunt in the history of the World is about to begin. The Government has set up a new department called Rat Control and they're hoping to start operations in this city. They've begun of course with posters and propaganda. Considering that Jones hasn't been dead a week yet they've acted very quickly. 'Commendable promptitude,' the paper calls it. Of course they had to. It's all right having a few children bitten by rats in the slums, but to have a prosperous businessman eaten alive on his own premises! There's been a public outcry. Of course this city is the obvious place for 'Operation Annihilation' to begin.

Everyone loves playing at soldiers.

The girl has heard that 'The Operation', as it's being called for short, will begin in our office—and in the warehouse too of course, the whole premises. They're going to seal the building off from the outside and fill it with gas. This is to happen next week-end.

At the same time I, at home, shall be playing my own small part in the National Effort. Secret Service. Lonely, unrecognised work, totally unremunerated.

I thought I was going to have to buy wire-netting. Fortunately I remembered that there was still a bit left in the front hedge—part of what Father had to keep out the dogs. My past consideration is paying off. I provided nesting boxes for all the rats which had litters. These are loose and can be carried about quite easily. All I have to do is to tack wire netting over the top of the boxes, leaving it turned back at one corner so that the rats can get in and out. I can do this without disturbing them. They are quite accustomed to me working at their boxes.

This morning we cremated the skull. I say, 'We,' because I attended with the rest. They used a coffin of the normal size, as if the whole of Jones was inside it. It was funny to think of just the skull, with the little bit of scalp and the dried blood, all alone in the big coffin.

The Senior Traveller and the Book-keeper were asked back to the house afterwards. Of course they didn't ask *me*. I wasn't thought sufficiently important. It makes me laugh when I remember that I am the most important person in the whole affair. Without me there wouldn't have been any funeral! Perhaps of course Mrs. Jones doesn't like me. How unreasonable of her! How right!

Saturday. I know the girl thinks I should have taken her for a run in the car. That's what I would have liked to do. But first things first. I told her, 'I really must work in the garden.' She didn't say, 'What about Sunday afternoon?' But I could see her thinking it. However I left it at that. All I'd said was perfectly true. And when you want to deceive it's best to stick to the truth. She may feel a bit sore, but she won't risk throwing me over just for that. She can get her revenge after we're married. If what people tell you's right I expect she will.

I had my lunch as usual. I always take a proper lunch on Saturdays and Sundays now. I think it's good for me, after sandwiches all week. I had stewed meat, boiled potatoes and boiled cabbage. I use one of these pressure cookers. It saves a lot of time. For my second course I had rice pudding with plenty of sugar and milk. I took my time over it. If I do heavy work straight after a meal it always gives me a headache. So I read a book for a bit before washing up. Then I changed into my gardening clothes and went out.

I thought I'd better bury them pretty deep. There's no knowing what notion the girl may take about gardening after we're married and I wouldn't want her coming on a lot of rat bodies if she starts to dig. She'd want to know why they were there. I've no idea how long they'll take to rot away. So I decided to dig a very deep hole, far deeper than she or any gardener would ever go. Digging a deep hole is much harder work than I realised. After I got about a spade depth down I came on a layer of small stones packed tightly together. I could hardly get the spade through it. Eventually I had to use a pick. And after the small stones I came to clay with bigger stones, almost boulders. I was nearly giving up and trying somewhere else. Only I thought everywhere else would probably be just as bad. Anyhow I went on. But the result was I didn't get the hole deep enough to satisfy me till it was nearly dark. By this time I was beginning to feel hungry, but I determined to get the job done with before I had anything to eat.

So I went in for the rats. Then I remembered something else I needed. I went out again and found a stone weighing about three pounds. I put it into the first box where there was a mother rat and about nine young ones. I turned down the wire-netting so that none of them could get out. I tied a bit of old clothes-line round the box and lifted it up. Neither the mother rat nor the children seemed the slightest bit concerned. They were accustomed to me. I carried out the box and threw it into the rain-barrel. Because of the stone it sank immediately. But I didn't watch. I had kept hold of one end of the piece of clothes-line. I left it dangling down the outside of the barrel and went away. After five minutes I came back and hauled up the box. I peered in by the light from the kitchen window. They were all dead. At least I thought so. But I wasn't quite sure. One of the young ones seemed to twitch a little.

I threw the box back in. After ten minutes I came back again. No twitching this time. I carried the box to the hole. I turned up the wire netting, and standing over the hole shook the corpses into it. The stone fell in too. I had just meant to use the same stone for all the drownings, but I hadn't the courage to grovel among the corpses and find it again. So I got another stone for the next box. This time there was no sign of life.

Nine boxes in all. I used a separate stone for each. By the time I came to the last I'd had to do quite a bit of hunting round to find stones of the right size. Otherwise no trouble. I filled in the hole. It was very late. I brought the boxes into the kitchen to dry. Tomorrow I shall make a bonfire and burn them all.

So now I have no rats.

I put on one egg to boil for my tea. Usually I have two, but somehow I didn't feel as hungry as I had earlier on.

More dreams. All horrible.

This morning the boxes were quite dry. I made a heap of them in the garden with everything else that had ever had to do with the rats. I stuck in a lot of old newspapers and set the whole alight at three different points. It made a great blaze, but it didn't last long. Then I went through the house from top to bottom and picked up every bit of rat dirt I could find. Actually I couldn't find very much. Only Socrates and Ben had had the run of the house and they were both pretty careful. Next I went round sprinkling disinfectant over everything. I couldn't smell anything myself, but you never know. Someone else might.

It's nearly bedtime. I feel content. No rats. No sign of rats. I might be anyone. A bachelor. Still quite young. Left alone since his poor mother died. Recently come into a bit of money. Contemplating matrimony. A good catch for some lucky girl. Of course it's going to be. . . . Well, you know who. All I have to do now is put the question. I have no doubt what the answer will be.

At about eleven o'clock this morning the Book-keeper and the Senior Traveller, both looking very important, asked me into Jones's private office—really Father's old office. Though what right *they* have to it I don't really know. After a great deal of beating about the bush it turned out that they wanted me to take over Jones's interest in the business. They must know about my legacy. Perhaps Jones had told Mrs. Jones, and Mrs. Jones had told *them* after the funeral. It doesn't matter really. There is now no particular reason why it should remain secret.

At any rate when they went back to the house after the funeral the future of the business was discussed. Mrs. Jones wanted to sell out. They thought of me. None of the others has enough money to take over. Not that they actually admitted that to me.

I bet they all think I'm the very person they're looking for. Not much good at business. Easy to deal with. I expect Mrs. Jones thinks I'll give more than the shares are worth just for the sake of getting back the family firm. The other two, the Senior Traveller and the Book-keeper, probably imagine that once I become the major shareholder they will be able to do what they like, that I shall be clay in their hands. They think I'm soft. They'll learn the truth in due course. Or some of it. I shall drive a hard bargain with Mrs. Jones. As for the Book-keeper and the Senior Traveller they'll soon see who's Boss.

Tonight I took the girl out to dinner. I meant to do the thing well, but the cost, £4 2s. 6d. exceeded my expectations. However I am now in a position to be extravagant on occasions. Not that I shall be extravagant very often and I am quite sure the girl would not wish it any more than I should. If I thought otherwise I should not have done what I have.

After dinner we returned to the car. I drove a short distance and then turned into a quiet side road. I parked the car under a tree with two wheels on the grass verge. I turned off the headlights, but left on the sidelights (and of course the rear lights) so that no one would run into us.

I said, 'Will you marry me?'

She said, 'Yes.'

After that I would hardly have known what to do, but the girl immediately kissed me on the mouth. So of course I kissed her. A most delightful sensation, quite different from kissing Mother goodnight. We continued kissing in this manner, just our lips meeting, for some time, till it occurred to me to put my arms round her and draw her close to me. This proved even more pleasurable, with its intimations of still greater delights to come after we are actually married. We are both agreed that we should be married quite soon. I have left it to her to 'Name The Day.'

I have taken the girl over the house. I know she has been longing to see inside ever since we first became friendly. I bet she's looked at it from the outside often enough, though you can't see much from the road.

I made a sort of apology for it before I actually let her in to explain why I had never shown it to her before. I said, 'I'm afraid it's all a bit of a mess and you'll find the furniture pretty old and decrepit.' This in spite of the fact that I'd gone to great pains to tidy everything up, and that the furniture's just the same as it always was. I mean if it was good enough for Father and Mother—and Grandfathers and Grandmothers some of it—why shouldn't it be good enough for her. I expected her to admire it in fact, but she said nothing. At last I remarked, 'I expect you'd like it refurnished from top to bottom.' Our whole future trembled in the balance.

She answered, 'Oh Darling, you couldn't think of doing that. It would be far too expensive. Besides I'm sure you love these dear old things. They must have so many associations for you.'

How strangely the mind works. Immediately I felt an urge to get rid of everything, even the house itself. 'I don't care about the associations,' I told her. 'When we get married I want life to start afresh. We'll sell this house if you like and go and live somewhere else.'

'Oh no!' she exclaimed. 'I think it's a lovely house. I'd hate you to sell it. It just needs doing up.'

There's something about the house. It exercises its fascination on everyone who knows it. From the moment Father died Jones longed to possess it. Mother and I lived on the verge of poverty rather than give it up, while later I almost starved myself to keep it from falling into Jones's hands. The girl was right. I might feel repugnance at its associations, but I couldn't leave it. If we re-furnished and re-decorated the associations would be banished— Father's dominance, Mother's inquisitiveness, her insistence on always knowing where I was going, Socrates whom I had betrayed,

Ben who had forced himself on me. . . . Paper, paint and new furniture would sweep away all these ghosts.

'I'll leave it in your hands,' I said. 'Don't ruin me. That's all.'

'How much can I spend?' she asked. She's intensely practical.

'A thousand,' I offered.

'A thousand?' She looked doubtful.

I was surprised, but I remembered the fearful cost of everything these days. I had no wish to appear parsimonious. 'Two thousand,' I suggested.

She thought for a moment. Then she threw her arms round my neck. 'Darling, you're sweet. I won't let it cost as much as that and I think we might get quite a bit back on the old furniture.'

I am so happy I could sing for joy. A complete new life of freedom and love. The past wiped out as if it had never existed.

When I had the bonfire I forgot about the rat-head mask. I must try to get rid of it at the week-end.

The girl is amazingly efficient. She organises everything. She arranged with an auctioneer to inspect my furniture. We met at the house during our lunch hour today. She drove out with the auctioneer. I went in my own car. This was because our engagement is still secret from the staff in the office. The girl thinks it best to keep it so till my negotiations for the purchase of the shares have been completed. That I am about to buy the shares is, however, no secret. As a result I am treated in the office in quite a new way, that is to say with great respect. If I return half-an-hour late after the lunch break, no one asks where I've been.

The auctioneer is quite enthusiastic about my furniture—so enthusiastic indeed, that for a moment my resolution wavered. Had I not made a terrible mistake in agreeing to part with it? Then I looked at the girl and I thought of the new life we were going to have together, a new life in what would be virtually a new house. I saw that I wanted everything to be fresh and clean and bright. I didn't want to live with her among the old, red plush upholstery, the tassels on the chairs, or to make love in a rattly iron bed, ornamented with tarnished brass knobs.

'Victoriana,' the auctioneer calls it. He says it has become very fashionable. He is most anxious that the auction shall be in the house itself. Everything will sell better in its natural setting. I'm quite sure he is right. So I agreed at once. There will be one locked room where we will put anything we want to keep out of the auction—my clothes, for instance. 'Personal effects,' the auctioneer called them. I had a feeling that at any moment he might refer to me as 'The deceased.'

My negotiations with the Jones family are proceeding smoothly. They are working through a solicitor and on the advice of the girl so am I. Also on her advice I am only offering to purchase fifty-one per cent of the shares now, with an option to purchase the remainder in four years' time at the same price. As she points out fifty-one per cent will give me control so that I can fix my own salary. If the business does well the shares will be worth a good deal more in four years, but I won't have to pay any more for them. If the business does badly, or indifferently, I can leave them alone or else negotiate a better price. In either case I shall have enough capital left outside the business to allow us to live in reasonable comfort.

The auction was a terrific success. I had no idea our old furniture was worth anything like as much, and in fact a year or two ago it wouldn't have been. It's just that everything we had has suddenly come into fashion. Just one example. The china from the spare bedroom—two basins, two water jugs, two things for holding toothbrushes, two soap dishes and two chamber-pots—fetched seven pounds ten shillings. The people just seemed to go mad. I heard quite a respectable looking young woman say that the chamber-pots would be used as punch bowls. Well of course they haven't been used much, but they have been used. . . . I certainly wouldn't fancy having to drink anything that came out of them.

I am writing this in the bedroom of my hotel. I locked up the house as soon as the last of the furniture had been taken away, and moved in here. That was about an hour and a half ago. I was afraid to leave the house unoccupied any sooner. I've been nervous ever since the first advertisements appeared in the local papers. They seemed to be just asking thieves to break in and steal—specially when you remember that I was away at business all day. I am going to go on living here, or in some other hotel if I find I don't like this one, till all the alterations at home are finished. I shall move in again before the new furniture is delivered. To be more precise. . . . We are going to furnish the spare bedroom first. I shall then move in and occupy it while the rest of the house is being re-furnished. On the day of our marriage an aunt of the girl's will come in and live in the house while we are away on our honeymoon. You just can't be too careful these days. Of course the aunt will move out as soon as we get home.

After all I still haven't destroyed the rat-head mask. So much of my spare time has been taken up with the girl that I never seemed to get round to it. It's in a locked trunk in the locked room. It's safe enough there meantime. I'll have to get rid of it before we're married. If there was a locked trunk in the house it would be the very thing she'd want to see into. She'd open it somehow or other.

This morning, at the office of the Jones solicitors, the share trans-fer giving me control of the business was completed. My solici-tor was also present. We handed over a cheque and in return I received a certificate for the shares. I was then elected a director of the Company and at once appointed Managing Director. The Book-keeper and the Senior Traveller were elected Directors. The Book-keeper was also appointed Secretary of the Company. Mrs. Jones and Miss Jones resigned their directorships.

Immediately I got back to the office I transferred all my belong-ings to the Managing Director's office, i.e. Father's old office, lat-terly Jones's office. As soon as I felt comfortably settled in I sent for the Book-keeper. I told him that the girl would take over my duties as Cashier pro-tem, but that he should make immediate arrange-ments to engage someone else to fill the position on a permanent basis.

'Do you not think she could take it over on a permanent basis?' he asked, meaning the girl of course.

'No,' I said. 'That would not be suitable.' I gave no further explanation. He went out looking rather puzzled. This of course has all been arranged between her and me. She will carry on the Cash for a few weeks, till in fact the new Cashier has been thor-oughly trained in his job and can carry on alone. She will then give in her notice. On the day she actually leaves there will presumably be the usual little office party with a small presentation from the staff—she hasn't been in the firm long enough for it to be very large. At this party we shall announce our engagement. Terrific surprise. Congratulations all round. I don't think anyone has any idea.

It's not all fun being Managing Director. This evening the Senior Traveller knocked on my office door about half an hour before locking-up time. I knew who it was almost before he was in the door and looked up with a kindly, but tired expression. 'What can I do for you?' I enquired, pleasantly condescending.

'It's about this business of being a director,' he said. 'What do I get out of it?'

I hadn't intended him to get anything out of it. The girl and the Solicitor had both advised me to make these two directors, but I hadn't been a bit keen. I know quite a lot about directors. Once a man becomes director of a firm he gets ideas of grandeur and needs more salary to keep up his new position. It was different for me. In taking over Jones's position I naturally took over his salary, but all that was wanted of the Senior Traveller and Book-keeper was that they should just carry on. However the Senior Traveller is very popular with the customers and I didn't wish to fall out with him in any way.

'Do sit down,' I said, oozing cordiality, but really just to gain time.

He sat down. 'I just want to know what's in this for me.'

I had a frivolous temptation to answer, 'Nothing, I hope,' but I fought it back. 'It will improve your position,' I told him, 'make you more secure.' I tried to think how the girl would advise me to deal with this situation.

'I'm not worrying about security,' he said. 'How much more money am I going to get?' He stuck out his chin and stared at me across the desk. I'd often heard him say that he had determined not to leave such an' such a customer without an order. I felt just as if I was one of these customers. I didn't like it a bit.

His eyes were still boring into me. I suddenly remembered. Play for time. 'I'll have to think about it,' I replied.

'How long do you need to think?'

'Oh! Well I suppose about a week.'

'All right. I'll expect an answer this day week.' He got up and went out.

It's not much good being 'The Boss', if you get treated like that. I'll get back on him some day.

The house is coming on very well. The only really big changes are a second bathroom, with W.C., and a door from the kitchen straight into the dining room. What is making such a difference to the house is the modernisation, new bath and basin in the old bathroom, new sink in the scullery, and then everything re-papered and painted in light colours. You'd hardly know the house. It looks so bright and cheerful.

We've spent a lot on furniture, but what we got for the old stuff has gone a long way towards paying for the new. After all I'm not going to be out of pocket more than about £1,400, which is much better than I'd begun to expect. The girl has a real money sense.

She says she might want to put in a third bathroom later if there are children, but that can wait. We both want children, but we feel it would be tempting Providence, to put in a bathroom for them until we know that the first child is at least on the way.

I had another dream about Jones last night. He said the business was still his. Even when I awoke I couldn't get him out of my mind.

I've had to give the Senior Traveller an extra hundred a year and the Book-keeper an extra fifty, with the promise of a bonus if we have a good year. If the whole staff start asking for rises my profit is going to be cut. I don't see why they can't be satisfied with what they got when Jones was boss.

I'm moving back home on Saturday. The wedding is this day four weeks. As soon as I get a bit of time to myself I really must burn that mask.

Back home. Such comfort! We've got an immersion heater as well as everything else. Hot water any hour of the day or night. I'm so busy with one thing and another that I've no time to write in my notebook. I never seem to be alone. I mean it's after my usual bedtime when I say 'Goodnight,' to the girl. By the time I get home myself I'm too tired to do anything but just fall into bed. She's going away next week and I'm really quite looking forward to it. She's to stay with a friend in London, starting on Monday afternoon, and coming back the following Monday. She finishes at the Office on Friday. She gave in her notice to the Book-keeper about ten days ago. Of course I pretended to be surprised when he told me. 'I thought she was very happy here,' I remarked.

'I think she's going to get married,' he said.

'Is that so?' I replied, smiling benevolently.

Since I have become Managing Director I have naturally had to alter my manner with the staff, the girl included. No more soup at lunch-time. I go out to quite a good restaurant. I have to consider my position. Once we are married I shall go home. A restaurant is really too expensive for every day, though going home in the car will cost quite a lot too.

Still these horrible dreams. Every night I have them. Sometimes Jones. Sometimes the rats. Sometimes both together.

Tonight I'm alone at home. So restful just to sit at the fireside by myself and write my notes. I don't mean I'm not looking forward to the time when the girl is sitting opposite, maybe doing her knitting, all nice and cosy, just the two of us. . . . Or maybe she'll be out in the kitchen, bustling about, washing-up perhaps, though she should be finished by this time.

The only thing is I won't be able to sit like this writing my notes. Sure as fate she'd be leaning over me. 'What's that you're writing, Darling?'

'And you've been keeping notes all this time and never told me?'

'Oh that was very naughty of you! You'll have to show me them all, right from the very beginning.'

And she'd make me. She's very strong willed. The only way to oppose her is by subterfuge. What she'd be looking for, of course would be me writing down how beautiful she was. 'My love is like a red, red rose,' and all that sort of guff. It's not just that she wouldn't find what she was looking for. It's what she would find.

I wonder what she'd do. It's funny. I haven't an idea. So I won't take any chances. I'll buy a special deed-box, of which I'll keep the key myself, and leave it in the safe-deposit in the Bank with all my old notebooks inside. I don't care what anyone finds out about me after I'm dead. I expect that if I do have children they'll burn the lot. Save a scandal. 'To think that Father was that awful Ratman!' 'Don't tell poor Mother. I'm sure she never had any idea.' And of course she won't have. Not if *I* can help it.

Of course if I'd just a little more sense I'd burn the lot myself, but there's something about something you've written. I mean it's yourself, isn't it? And then suppose even your children found it, and didn't destroy it. They might think it was too interesting to destroy. They'd lock it up again and say, 'Oh well it would be no harm in letting this be known in a hundred years' time, when we're all dead. By that time it's not going to matter to anyone.' Then in a hundred years' time it would come out and go to a museum as an historical document. Parts of it might even be published.

'GREAT TWENTIETH CENTURY MYSTERY SOLVED AT LAST
The story of Ratman, who terrorised . . .'

Something like that. Perhaps with my photograph. I must get my photograph taken and put it in the box. You never know. My family mightn't bother to keep my photograph. I remember after Father died Mother threw out a lot of old photographs of *his* relations.

I'll buy the deed-box tomorrow.

The most awful thing has happened. Ben is alive. Not only is he alive. He's here, now, in this room watching me. He's not alone either. The cellar's full of rats again. Not all the rats I set out with when I went to kill Jones. But some of them, and a lot of others I never saw before. Not furry-tails at all, just a gather-up, miscellaneous rats Ben has fallen in with on the way here. He's lost his sense of racial discrimination, or class consciousness. 'A rat's a rat for a' that,' he says to himself, and doesn't care any more whether tails are worn scaly or furry.

It's no sense joking all the same. I'm in a hole, and I don't quite know how to get out of it. The girl will be home on Monday.

I came back from the office today, gay as a lark. I put the car in the garage, picked up the deed-box all wrapped in paper and string, and proceeded towards the front door. I looked in the sitting room window as I passed and there was Ben on the back of the sofa. I stopped dead. He saw me. For a bit we just looked at each other through the glass. He's as thin as a rake, and all the others are as thin as he is. At that point I didn't know about the others. I thought it was just Ben. There's no doubt what they've come for. Food. Ben and his lot look as if they haven't had a good meal since they finished up Jones. And the gather-up they've brought with them probably haven't had a good meal ever.

I thought of a lot of things as I stood there. I've got so accustomed to not having the rats that it was almost as if I'd *never* had them. I was like any ordinary citizen arriving home and finding a rat in the parlour. The ordinary citizen has his instructions staring at him from every hoarding in the city. 'At first sign of rats, telephone the police and ask for Rat Destruction. Don't try to deal with them yourself. Even if you only see one, there may be more which you can't see. Remember! Rats Kill!'

But if I 'phoned Rat Destruction they'd be out like a swarm of bees. They'd be over the whole place, looking for rats. And they might find my rat-head mask, and they might find my notebooks.

Suddenly I had a flash. Why not poison him? You can get poison. It's free as a matter of fact. They give it to you at the Centre. People put it down who haven't rats at all, just in case. It's the public-spirited thing to do. Major Robinson has bait down all over his garden, though he says he's never seen a rat within a mile of it. They've passed a law making it an offence if you have rats not to report them. This is because, in spite of all the danger, a lot of people don't like to report they have rats. They're afraid of getting a bad name among the neighbours for being dirty or something.

I thought to myself, 'Surely I can put up with Ben for one night. I've put up with him plenty of nights before.' So I unlocked the door and went inside.

'Hello, Ben,' I said. 'You've been away a long time.' I put out my hand to stroke him, but he snapped at me.

I went back to the hall and hung up my coat and hat in the

cloakroom. Things didn't seem just too bad. I could surely deal with Ben by himself. But something made me open the cellar-door and go down there. It was full of rats. They looked at me, all this starved lot of them, just as if it might have been a lot of cannibals looking at their next meal. I couldn't get up the steps and the door shut quick enough. One thing was very clear. I'd have to get it into their heads that I was the meal-provider, not the meal.

I shot straight out, not going back to Ben in the sitting room. Outside the front door I stopped to think again. Would I not be better after all to phone Rat Destruction? It was going to be a risk going back in there. Then I thought again of the mask, and the notebooks.

I got out the car and started on a round of shops that stay open after the usual shop-hours. I bought two loaves in the first. But I thought they looked at me rather. So in the next I just bought one, and in the next and the next, and the next. . . . When I thought I'd enough I went home. I'd got a bit of cold boiled ham for Ben. He'd always been fond of cold ham, but usually I hadn't let him have any—just if I'd some over and it looked like going a bit mouldy. However the thing just now was to appease him. I needn't have bothered. He'd appeased himself in the larder without considering his friends and relations. What's more he's lost his manners. There was rat dirt over everything. Perhaps he's just showing me he doesn't care any more. The result was I kept the bit of ham and part of one of the loaves for myself as there was nothing in the larder I cared to touch. I flung the remaining loaves down into the cellar and the rats were on them like a pack of wolves.

So here I am watching Ben, and Ben watching me. He could kill me during the night, but I don't think he will. He wants to keep me for the sake of a comfortable home. He knows that without me the food won't come rolling in, and by the look of him I should think he's had enough of foraging for himself. I'll buy grain tomorrow and I'll mix poison with it. By the next day they should all be dead. If there are any half dead I should be able to finish them off with a spade or something. It's wonderful how desperation gets rid of squeamishness.

Tomorrow in the office I think I'd better tell them I won't be in the following day. If all goes well I'll be conducting a mass funeral and I don't want anyone coming out to see what's happened to me.

Now I'm in the attic—putting in time
    Till what?
    Well they're doing nothing yet
    I wish to heavens I hadn't told the office I wouldn't be in tomorrow. I wish I'd told them instead to come and look for me if I wasn't in at the usual time. Even that mightn't have been any good. I wish I'd never come home tonight. But I did. I brought the grain and the poison.
    When I got in I went straight to the sitting room. I don't know why. Ben was on the table this time, my notebook open in front of him. He cocked his head sideways so that one eye was fixed on what I had written and the other was half-watching me. Then he gave a kind of shake to his head as if to say, 'I've read it all. *I* know what you're up to.'
    I made a grab and got the notebook. Ben jumped off the table and on to a chair. From that on to the floor and under the sofa. I came up here. Meant to get the mask and the deed-box with all the notebooks. Then clear out.
    Not quick enough. The rats had come up after me. A solid mass of them crossing the landing. Just got the door shut in time.
    I can't reach the skylight. Too high. Have to sit out and hope.
    Leave that door alone, damn you.
    They'd gnaw the door down if I didn't keep yelling. Maybe somebody will hear me

That is all. Not even a full stop. The remaining pages in the last notebook are blank. Among them however I did find a loose sheet of paper. On it was written in a different hand from the rest, the following:
    'There can't be much doubt as to what happened. Ratman stopped writing. Either he expected an immediate assault from the rats, or else for the time being he had no more to say. He put the notebook into the deed-box with the other notebooks, and locked the box. Whether he then made an attempt to break out, or whether the rats broke into the room we have no means of knowing. But I think his fate was the same as the fate of Jones: only this time the rats had more time and were more thorough.

There was no skull to put in a coffin, no hair, no drops of blood on the floor, just the empty room with the locked metal box and the notebooks inside.

'That was what the police found.

'I had the utmost difficulty in getting them to part with the note-books—but after all, I am the next-of-kin.

'Now I don't know what to do. As a family we are not anxious to advertise our relationship to Ratman—though the connection is very dis-tant. At the same time I think the notebooks must have a certain scientific importance and for that reason deserve publication, in part at least.'

CPSIA information can be obtained
at www.ICGtesting.com
Printed in the USA
LVHW040740201218
600894LV00003BB/366/P